The Lincoln High Project

by Raelee May Carpenter

Big Break Publishing Company, LLC
Mason, MI

Big Break Publishing Company, LLC 721 West Barnes Road Mason MI
48854 USA bigbreakpub@juno.com

Cover design by Jeremiah Tear. Interior design by Rachel Tear. Edited by
Amy Parker and Rachel Tear.

~for Ricky

Prologue –

The scene: Shadows. That's all I really remember now; I think that's most of what I saw then. Blurry shadows and my bare feet, spotted with blood, my blood. That's all I could see through the rag over my eyes. I think we were in the basement, but I couldn't tell you for sure. All I could see was shadows and my bloody feet…

Why is he doing this again? I tried to be good. I don't know what I did. I didn't break anything. I did what he told me to - everything he told me to. What did I do? Why are they hurting me again?

"What's the big deal?" she says.

Who is she, anyway?

"I can only explain away so many bruises they can see," he says.

With this on, I can't even see what's coming next. Where it will hurt next.

She says, "Tell them he fell down the stairs."

He says, "He's 'fallen down the stairs' dozens of times in the past four years. They finally made me promise to keep the door locked."

"Well…"

"You know, probably no one would miss him if-"

"Wait!"

"We could just tell them he ran away. He's done that. And who'd expect a nine-year-old kid to survive on his own very long?"

"When they found him, they'd be able to tell he was beaten up. You'd be the first suspect; the guardians always are. Even if they didn't figure it out, they'd probably charge you with negligence."

"Then I would never get another kid… See All The Trouble YOU'VE STUCK Me With, STUPID KID!! You Better Run! Tuck, Duck, And Roll, Moron!"

Owww…my stomach. Can't breathe. Not gonna cry, though. That'll only make him madder, make it worse. Oh, air…

If only I knew where I was for sure, I could go sit on the stairs or something and just watch…watch them beat up the blond kid with the speech impediment.

"Nobody would miss this kid," he says. "I'm telling you, he's worthless. His own parents didn't even want him."

"Yeah, but he belongs to the State now. You gotta be careful with State property."

"They don't care. He costs them money."

"Some people get that job because they care about trash like him."

"But he's worthless!"

Maybe Mrs. Jones could come and sit with me. She could sit with me and watch them hurt the blond-haired boy with the speech impediment, who she thinks fell down the stairs dozens of times. Then she'd know.

"Yeah, but-" she starts.

"No one cares," he interrupts.

That wasn't fair. Mrs. Jones cared about the little boy. Well, she cared about him as much as anyone could care about any number – any number with blond hair, blue eyes, and a speech impediment.

"But they still have to act like they do."

"All over a WORTHLESS KID!"

OWW!!! Mrs. Jones disappears, and the stairs. The shadows and bloody feet are back. So is the pain. But I'm not gonna cry. He'll stop...eventually.

Then one more hit, and there are no shadows. No bloody feet. Just darkness.

*****

"...going to be okay?"

I was waking up, slowly. Blurry voices cleared, and dull pain became keen.

"You got to him in time. He should be okay physically. Emotionally...probably not so much. Though you've been a social worker so long, I probably don't have to tell you that."

"I've seen enough of this over the years, but we're usually taking them from those homes, not putting them in. After four years with that monster, this one will not be in good condition."

Mrs. Jones...Where am I?

"Even after all your experience, it must be difficult to see."

"He was a sweet kid when I met him, scared and alone, but sweet. Not after this. I wouldn't be surprised if he turned into a similar type of monster himself." She sighs. "It's probably about time for me to retire. Anyway, thanks for your help, doctor."

I open my eyes, but the light is sharp, so I close them again.

"It's my job. I'd rather have mine than yours. But he's waking, so I'll leave you alone with him now."

Chapter one ~

Ever hear people tell stories about how much they loved high school? You won't hear me telling stories like that. Ever read one of those books about how great high school is? This isn't one of those books. High school wasn't exactly a great time for me. There were good things; I mean, I had my family, my friends, and I saw some beautiful things happen. But I lived through my share of nightmares too. It's an interesting story, but when I decided to write it, it wasn't easy to know where to start. I didn't want to bore you with too many details, but I didn't want to skip something you needed to know. I finally supposed this was as good a time as any…

"So I can come over tonight?" Mark Ross, my longtime best friend and life-long neighbor asked me. He closed his locker door and shifted his feet, scuffing the toes of his red high tops on the linoleum.

"Sure, but you'll have to get the movies. I have to take Shannon to her piano lesson after I pick her and Andy up from school. I won't get home until after five. Then I'll have to eat dinner, clean up the dishes, clean my room-"

"Okay, Annie Eire. I get the point. I'll have the movies."

"Can you pay for them this time? I have an interview at the mall toy store on Monday, but my current life's work of babysitting Shannon and Boyne Andrew doesn't pay." I wrinkled my nose. "Though it should."

"Shannon and Andy gave you a lot of trouble last weekend, huh, Aine?"

(Yeah, Aine - pronounced ÄN-yuh - is my actual name. It's the Irish Gaelic translation of Anna.)

"I already told you about last weekend," I reminded Mark.

"I was suppressing."

"And you didn't even have to live it."

"What can I say? I'm a sensitive guy."

I know that's a line a lot of guys use on girls without it having any basis in reality whatsoever. In Mark's case, even though he jokes about it, it's true. He is sensitive and sweet and a perfect gentleman. He's also a computer genius – though he dresses more skate-punk than preppie-nerd. Also, like me, Mark Ross is a member of "The Lincoln High School Outcast Club." Yeah, we're not popular, but it's not an easy thing to tell just by looking at us. You have to know Lincoln High to be able to figure out who's on the in and who's on the out. So let me teach you about Lincoln High.

It's not our looks. Mark and I aren't drop-dead gorgeous or anything, but we're not hideous, either. Mark's a little skinny, and I have a few charming freckles on my nose. Some members of the in-group are less attractive than us.

It's not about money. My father's a surgeon, and Mark's dad is a businessman, and our families do well. But we're not too well off to be popular, because Lincoln serves a smaller and richer area than Port Morgan's other three high schools. I suspect a sort of gerrymandering was happening when the district drew the lines many decades ago, but in Lincoln High terms, our upper middle class families are pretty average financially.

It's not about intelligence either. Mark and I are smart, but not too smart. Lincoln's clientele tends to run just on the low side of what educators call "gifted". That puts me right on the peak of the bell curve, and Mark a bit off to the smart side. Popular kids sit on every area of that curve.

With Mark, it's not about skin color. Black and white is one thing that's never mattered a hill of beans here. And with me, it's not that I'm first generation American, with parents who lived in Ireland until they were about six. Most people have never met my parents, let alone viewed their birth certificates, but I don't think it would matter to my classmates if they did know.

I mean, sure, all of the above has its own weight in the matter, but just a bit. They're not the Deciding Factor. The Deciding Factor is-

"Do you wanna invite Ben and Juliana?" Mark asked me, breaking into my thoughts.

"Yeah. Can you call them?"

He smiled, rubbing a hand quickly over his short, curly black hair. "Sure." Our friends, Ben Wilson and his girlfriend Juliana Huntington are average in every area, even the Deciding Factor. Except in friendship. With Mark, Ben, and Juliana, I couldn't have picked better friends if I'd held open auditions.

"So, I'll see you later?" Mark asked me.

"Yeah. Tonight. My house."

By the way, The Deciding Factor, the test of all things popular at Lincoln High School, is athletic ability. Beating Ford High is very important here.

I was about to head out to the parking lot when a high-pitched, squeaky, yet popular voice pierced the din of the crowded hallway. "Hey, Ae-nee!"

That is definitely not how my name is pronounced. I looked back at Mark. "Please tell me there's someone here whose name is actually pronounced like that."

He frowned and shook his head. "No, sorry."

"Then it's one of their secret nicknames for someone?"

"Hey!" the screech shattered the air again. "Aee-nee O'Brien!"

"Sorry, kid. She's talking to you."

"You know, if we were in Ireland, she'd shout that surname in a crowded hallway and I'd bet fifty kids would turn around."

Mark shrugged. "We're in Michigan, and I'm getting out of here. Vanessa Montgomery isn't my idea of a pleasant conversation."

"So you think I'm excited about that exact prospect?" I returned with an incredulous tone.

He gave me his palms up, lower lip drooped, eyebrows raised, sorry-it's-just-not-my-problem look.

"Please, Mark, take me with you."

He snorted a laugh. "No can do, but, I'll tell you what. I'll drive T.J. up the street from the middle school, thus enabling a quick escape."

"Thanks a lot. Some friend you've turned out to be."

He grinned at me, and I couldn't help smiling back.

"Aeee-neeee Ooooh' Briiii-ennnn!"

My smile turned into a teeth-baring cringe.

"Bye!" He hollered at me as he disappeared around the corner.

"Hey, Ae-nee!" Vanessa greeted me as she approached.

"I'm sorry," I said. "It took me awhile to figure out you were talking to me."

Vanessa gave me a puzzled look. "Why?"

"Because my name is pronounced Än'- yuh."

12

"Right. Anyway, I need to talk with you for just a moment, Ae-nee!"

"Än'-yuh."

"What's the big deal?"

"'Ae-nee' isn't my name. My name is Aine. You wouldn't like it if I started calling you 'Bob' or something."

"Whatever. Geez." Her long, shiny blond hair tossed, and her pale blue eyes rolled.

I glanced away from her because I couldn't stand her face; it was too perfect. "What was it that you wanted to tell me?" I asked. "I need to get going, so…"

"Right. Well, the committee for motivational speaking at the Junior Retreat wants you to do one of the talks!"

I groaned inwardly. Explanation? Like I said, Lincoln High is in a rich area. Well, several years ago said area decided that while the seniors got the two weeks in Hawaii for a Senior Trip, the juniors should get something too. So they came up with the Junior Retreat: "eight days and eight nights of relaxing, class bonding, and motivational speaking in beautiful, sunny Orlando, Florida." Yes, it sounds great, but I wasn't excited. This thing chokes down our entire spring break, which I usually would spend going someplace really cool with my family, like New York City or the Bahamas. Now, I was being asked to give one of the talks for the already-established program. Gag. Choke. Fidget. Cough.

"Which one?" I quizzed Vanessa.

"The fears and dreams one!"

Cough. Cough. Fidget. Gag. Choke.

"The one where they make you write your fears on the black paper and your dreams on the white paper and put them in those boxes?" I'd heard about that one. Big slice of Gouda.

"That's the one!" Her perpetually excited tone was making me sick. As if the talk wasn't bad enough, she had to act like it was All So Exciting.

"May I think about it?" I asked. If I had to give a talk, I would want to give the one on "respect for all classmates." But my school has never been brave enough to ask for an outcast's opinion on that.

"The thing is, I need to know now. Mr. Grenier, the lit teacher - he's the staff advisor for the talks - wants it that way so you can write the talk over the long Thanksgiving break!"

Right. My school was giving us a whole week off for Thanksgiving so they would have time to take the asbestos insulation out of the performing arts building (How they were allowed to keep it in thus far, I've no idea, but they "suddenly" needed to get it out).

"But I could decide during the Thanksgiving break and write it over Christmas, if I decided to do it," I told Vanessa.

"Well, Mr. Grenier wanted the Junior Retreat board to be able to review it during Christmas break. That way they can approve it, and you can make any necessary revisions in time for the retreat."

I felt totally put-on-the-spot, and I hate feeling put-on-the-spot. Also, happy tone aside, Vanessa didn't seem incredibly excited about asking me. I figured that even though I'm good at speeches, she'd already dismissed the idea of me doing a talk, because she doesn't like me. Someone had probably bailed on her at the last minute, and she was desperate to get her part of the retreat organized by Thanksgiving. I was a last resort. I sighed. "Fine. I'll do it."

"Great!" She looked like she was about to hug me for saving her life like I did, so I backed away quickly, muttering that I had to go. I'm not at all against being hugged, see - but I didn't want her to pretend even for a minute that I was one of her popular friends. I'm not at all athletic... "Bye, Ae-nee!"

...And my name hasn't helped either. "Bye, Bob," I muttered under my breath, because my Dad always told me to keep tight control of the volume of certain remarks. "Your annoyance will fade faster than the memory of your voice," he'd always said. "And certain words spoken too loudly may cause it to be difficult to make amends." He knows me well, my father does.

My father is Dr. Sean O'Brien, and my mom is his wife Kathleen. I'm almost seventeen, and my full name is Aine Erin O'Brien. I am the proud big sister of two brothers and a baby (don't tell her I call her that) sister. The older of my brothers (age thirteen, almost fourteen) is named Tierney Jay. The "Jay" is in his name simply because my parents decided to be merciful with him and paved the way to the nickname T.J. With my youngest brother and my sister, they got on an Irish river kick. **Boyne** Andrew (age ten) and **Shannon** Delaney (age seven). I missed bellbottoms by a decade, and the river thing is one more trend I'm glad I didn't get in on. Some of the other rivers in Ireland are called Liffey, Corrib, and Bride; and, quite frankly, I have enough trouble trying to explain Aine.

Don't get me wrong. My name's fine. It's just that…well, I want to be able to have a positive influence on my school; you know, help people here. Lincoln High is not an easy place to "shine;" and sometimes it seems my name is just one more thing that gets in the way of my…project, if you will. It frustrates me, and that frustration is enough to keep me repeatedly asking my mother, "Why on earth couldn't you have just called me Anna?"

Her answer's always the same, though. "Aine, *alannah*," she says with this little wistful smile on her face (By the way, *alannah* is Irish Gaelic for "my child."). "We Irish are a proud people."

Sure'n we love our heritage.

Chapter two –

Now, this is where my life gets interesting: J.D.

So I was just sitting in choir on the first day back from the long Thanksgiving break. And I was cold. The contractors had taken the asbestos insulation out of the fine arts building (technically "The Albert J. Kush and Rose M. Fielding Memorial Center for the Visual and Performing Arts at Abraham Lincoln Public High School," but who has time for all that?) and vacuumed the place and everything, so the building was "no longer a cancer risk." But they'd run out of time and had only begun to install the new insulation. The auditorium, the band room, and the dance studio were the only rooms that had insulation, leaving the drama room, the sculpture studio, the pens and paints studio, and the choir room sadly lacking. It wasn't a comfortable feeling, knowing that nothing but a speckled Styrofoam ceiling tile and a leaky aluminum roof separated me from the "wild, blue yonder."

I sighed, shivered, zipped-up my jacket, and pulled my hands into the sleeves. As I crossed my arms over my chest and shivered again, I reminded myself just how much I hated choir. I liked to sing, but the choir music was missing that likeable quality, the whatever-it-is that makes me like the music I do like.

Not too mention the un-insulated ceiling. I had been imagining creaks and moans coming from up in the ceiling all period. Then I heard it again, and I wasn't so sure it was my imagination. I gave another sigh/shiver as the director told us to stand up beside our desks. I stood slowly and, once standing, glanced at the suspicious spot in the ceiling, the spot directly over the little practicing platform. Temporarily satisfied that nothing was going on in the rafters, I stared at the platform at the front of room. See, staring through choir class is my form of passive resistance, protesting the dull music. I stared until I heard the noises again; then I was sure I hadn't imagined them.

I fixed my eyes on the suspicious spot. Another creak drifted down, and that was followed closely by a thud. Then, falling through the ceiling and landing on the platform in front of the shocked teacher's aide at the piano, came a body.

Chapter three-

I don't know why I did the next thing I did. I've always been squeamish about blood and that kind of thing. I believe blood has its place - in a hockey rink – other than that, seeing it tends to make me feel faint. That day it didn't matter. Without thinking, I vaulted towards the platform and knelt beside the boy who had blood matting his blond hair and seeping from his nose, mouth, and several other places on his body. I bent down beside his mouth to check for breathing. "Call 911," I shouted to no one in particular. "He's alive."

"We got a live one!" one of the jocks shouted, causing several others to laugh. I'd have slapped them all, had I not been more worried about the boy. As it were, I did yell at them. "Shut up! We're not talking about seafood! This is a human being!"

They gave me a condescending look, but they stopped laughing.

I turned all of my attention back to the boy; though, to say "boy" isn't exactly accurate. I was probably thinking of him that way because his situation made me feel protective, like I do about my youngest brother Boyne. The "boy," I realized, was probably about my own age. He was curled up in an instinctive, defensive pose; but I figured he had to be almost six-feet-tall with a slim but strong athletic build. He was unconsciousness; his pulse was steady, but slow and weak. "Hey," I called to him softly as I pushed hair away from a cut above his left eyebrow. "Can you wake up?"

He didn't respond, and I squeezed his shoulder and said, "Hang on, okay? We're getting you some help."

Mark came running into the classroom, carrying a first aid kit and a bottle of water. He'd been the one to go for help, I realized. Probably ninety percent of my choir class has cell phones in their pockets, and Mark who respects education too much to bring his to class had to run to use the payphone in the cafeteria. (One of my classmates did, however, have the presence of mind to call the local weekly newspaper.)

Mark joined me on the platform and set the water and first aid kit down next to me. I glanced at them, then looked the kid over. In addition to his face, his old t-shirt and carpenter jeans were stained with blood, but none of the bleeding seemed severe. Most of the blood seemed to be drying, actually. I decided I would work on waking him up and taking care of his face. The paramedics could take care of the rest of him. "What can I do?" Mark asked me.

"Would you try to get a splint on his finger?" I asked. "The right index finger; it looks broken. Check his feet and ankles." I nodded at the boy's old, black, combat boots. "It looks like his boots are almost off his feet, but be really careful when you slide them off the rest of the way."

"What do I use on the finger?" he asked.

"You could try a pencil or something. Gently, Mark," I repeated. "We don't want to cause more damage." Mark nodded and went to work taping the finger to a broken pencil from the floor. I opened the supply case, got some gauze, wet it with water from the bottle, and started wiping at the dried blood under the boy's nose. Mark came back to join me, and I looked and saw that even parts of the boy's old white socks were stained with blood. I turned away from the feet and concentrated on cleaning the blood away from his nose and mouth while Mark hung over my shoulder, watching.

"His feet are fine," Mark told me. "The bones at least, I mean. All the bleeding looks minor."

"Good," I responded.

"His lips aren't cut or anything," Mark commented as I finished with the blood by his mouth. "Where's that blood coming from?"

"Somewhere inside," I answered.

His eyes widened. "Internal injuries? Can you do something about that?"

"Yeah, I can, Mark." My tone was incredulous. "Dad and I covered the 'emergency surgery' chapter of *First Aid Made Easy* last week."

"Sorry. Duh."

I turned back to the first aid kit, drenched a cotton ball with rubbing alcohol, and pressed it to the cut above the kid's eyebrow. He finally reacted by reflexively bringing his arm up to shield his face. Mark pushed the arm away to give me a clear view of the cut, and the boy jerked, and his eyes shot open. He started to sit up. "No," I said, "don't move."

He seemed to consider my words and turned over onto his back instead. When he turned, I noticed a bruise under his right eye that was as dark as that grease paint some athletes wear; that had to be a day or two older than the other damage. His face tightened as he became aware of his injuries. He groaned softly, and his eyes started to close. "No!" I said. "Stay awake."

His eyes opened again and fixed on the ceiling. I followed his gaze and took in the hole from the missing tile, the bent metal framing, and the piece of plywood sitting precariously over the gap. When I glanced back at the boy, his eyes were closing again. "Hey, stay awake," I reminded.

His eyes slid over to look at me. "What's your name?" I asked. He blinked. "Do you remember it? What do people call you?"

He licked his lips and uttered a slurred response.

"Jadey?" I asked.

"Jay Dee," he told me.

"J.D.? Okay, J.D., what is that short for?"

"Dillon," he responded, his voice tight with pain. He didn't want to talk, but it would help him stay awake.

"Dillon? That's cool. What about the J.? Does that stand for something?"

"Yeah."

"What?"

"I...don't know."

"You don't know?" That was odd. Maybe he wasn't quite as lucid as I'd hoped. "J.D., are you in school? Where do you go to school?"

"Not here."

I knew that was the truth. As I tried to think of something else to ask, J.D.'s eyes began to close again. "Hey, J.D.," I called. "Stay awake."

He looked at me again. "I don't have a concussion," he told me. "He...I..."

"You were drugged?"

"Yes," he said in a choked voice.

"With what? Do you know?"

"Tylenol 3."

"Do you know how much?"

"A lot. Helped with the pain."

"What happened, J.D.? Who beat you up?"

He sighed and fought to keep his eyes open. "J.D., was it
someone you know?"

"Yes." He groaned. "I can't…"

"Okay, J.D. It's okay. Just hang on." He tried to take a
deep breath and was forced to wince for his effort; I wondered he
had a bruised or broken rib. "Hang on, okay? J.D.?"

"Okay," he murmured.

"That's good."

He tried to look optimistic. "It's…been worse."

That puzzled me. "That's…good," I said slowly. I smiled
reassuringly and put a hand on his shoulder. He cringed and jerked
away. I pulled back. "I'm sorry, J.D. Did that hurt?"

"No…I…" He swallowed hard and winced.

I decided it would be okay to give him a break. "It's fine," I
told him, reassuringly. "You don't have to talk anymore right now."
He let his eyes fall closed. A few seconds later, the paramedics
arrived, and Mark and I cleared away from him.

"What happened to him?" one of the paramedics asked us.

"He fell through the ceiling," one of the jocks answered,
stupidly. The paramedic gave the jock a brief, don't-intrude look.

"He looks like someone beat him up," I explained. "It seems to be mostly bruises and minor lacerations. One of his fingers looks broken. He seems to be experiencing pain in his chest when he breathes-broken ribs maybe. Probably check for internal injuries."

"Anything else?"

"He's been doped-up on oral codeine."

"Do you know how long he was in the ceiling?"

"No."

"Name?"

"J.D."

"Just J.D.?"

I nodded.

"Thanks," the paramedic told me before turning to J.D., who was lying on the dais with his face tight and his eyes half-open. "Okay, J.D.," he said, "we're going to fix you up. You'll be okay. How old are ya, J.D.?"

"About…seventeen," J.D. choked out.

"We'll make sure you see eighteen."

Chapter four –

I got to the hospital to see J.D. after school the next day. As I stood in the hall, carrying a card, a couple of balloons, and his boots, I said a prayer for wisdom, grace, and him. Then I took a deep breath and pushed through the door.

The room was semi-private, but the other bed was empty, and I smiled. My dad always says that he likes hospital beds best when they're empty; we thank God for empty beds. A woman in a suit was sitting in a brown, vinyl-upholstered chair next to J.D.'s bed. She'd been talking to him, but she hushed abruptly when I entered. I gave her a quick appraisal. Her face was perfectly made-up, and her legs were crossed demurely, but something I couldn't exactly describe about her made me uncomfortable.

J.D. was sitting on his bed, faced toward the door with his legs dangling off the side. The cut over his left eye had three stitches in it; the bruise under his right eye had faded a bit, and the blood had been washed from his blond hair. In addition to the standard, navy-print-on-white hospital gown, J.D. was wearing an old pair of black sweat pants with huge holes in the knees and a pair of worn but clean white socks. I could tell that his forearms, neck, knees, and probably much of his body I couldn't see, sported numerous scrapes and bruises.

When J.D. saw me his mouth and bright, blue eyes took on a sort of mildly-amused, guardedly-pleased expression. "Hey, Doctor-girl," he greeted. "When a nurse told me a few minutes ago that I had a friend on the way up, I had no idea what she meant. Hey," he said to the woman in the chair, "my hero is here."

The woman gave me a weak smile, and I gave her one considerably more cheerful. I handed J.D. the card, set the balloons on the night stand, and held up the plastic bag that contained his shoes. "I brought your boots," I told him. "They were left in the classroom."

"Thanks. I thought they'd cut 'em up."

"Do you want me to put them in the wardrobe for you?" I asked, nodding at the ubiquitous piece of basic, hospital-issue furniture.

"If you don't mind. I'm still not that mobile."

J.D. opened his card as I walked over to the wardrobe. While I was setting the shoes inside, I noticed an open duffel bag, stuffed full of well-worn clothes. The number of garments in the bag struck me as a little odd. J.D. was already sitting up and looking well, and it wouldn't be long before he'd be released - maybe a couple days. But he had enough clothes in the bag for a week, and he had stuff like jeans and collared shirts that one generally doesn't wear as a patient in a hospital. I pushed those thoughts out of my brain in a hurry and went back to J.D. He looked up from the card and said to me, "Aine O'Brien?" Except for underemphasizing the "r" in O'Brien, he pronounced my name exactly right. I was impressed.

"In the flesh," I told him, offering my hand for him to shake, but his gaze had returned to the card, so I turned and shook the woman's hand instead.

"I'm Ms. Keenan," she told me.

"Nice to meet you."

She opened her mouth to speak but was interrupted by the entrance of a doctor. The doctor went at J.D. with a stethoscope, and J.D. got this flicker of a look that, I imagine, was quite similar to the one he'd had when he was attacked the day before. He ducked away from the doctor, and Ms. Keenan touched the doctor's shoulder. The doctor leaned down to her, and she whispered something to him. Whatever she said confused him, but he turned back to J.D. and offered him the receiver end of the stethoscope. J.D. held the stethoscope to his own chest while the doctor listened to his heart and lungs. Then J.D. took his own blood pressure. The doctor gave J.D. a pill and left without completing the examination. When the doctor was gone, Ms. Keenan gathered her things and turned to J.D. "Think about what I said," she told him. "The choice is yours."

J.D.'s reply carried more than a tinge of sarcasm. "Because I actually have a choice."

I was confused. So he didn't have options? What were they talking about anyway?

She shrugged and said, "I'm sorry."

She didn't sound or look sorry at all. She left, and J.D. gave an involuntary but audible sigh. He gingerly lifted his legs onto the bed and used the remote to adjust it to the sitting-up position.

"That your mom?" I asked, nodding towards the doorway where Ms. Keenan had exited.

"No," he answered flatly, not offering any further explanation. A moment of awkward silence stole into the room, and I noticed J.D. was still holding my card, clutching it like found gold. I gave the room another look and realized my balloons and card were the only gifts or get well wishes. This was strange. Most teenagers in the hospital, especially ones like J.D. (who, lets face it, was an attractive, athletic-looking kid), would have their rooms covered in cards and gifts within an hour after their arrival. J.D. had nothing in his room more than twenty-four hours later. I promised myself I'd visit the next day with more goodies. I'd get a card from Mark. I'd bring some of those chocolates with all that random stuff inside them and a stuffed animal, something creepy, a lizard or snake, like my brothers like. Maybe-

"You're welcome to have a seat, Aine," J.D. said. "Um... I mean, if you want to stay awhile, that is." I looked at him as he continued, "You don't have to stay, if you don't want to; but, if you do, I don't mind. If you want to...stay, I mean."

Great. I'd been off in never-never land, and now J.D. thought I didn't want to visit with him. I had a feeling J.D. could use a visitor. Without a word, I plopped down into the old chair that had been vacated by Ms. Keenan. I planned on staying until someone kicked me out. "So," I said, once seated, "what's the diagnosis?"

He shrugged.

"Seriously," I prompted.

"Cuts and bruises, mostly. Three stitches over my left eye. Fractured rib - hairline, no big deal. Minor ulcer they cauterized. They did give me a blood transfusion, but it was mostly precautionary. They didn't have to waste the O-negative, because it's well-documented that I'm B-positive. One broken finger." He held up his right hand to show me that his index and middle fingers were taped together. "But it isn't bad. The speech impediment is not a mouth injury; I've had that forever." Well, the speech impediment explained his lazy r's and l's, but it was odd the way he rattled off his injuries in such a detached tone. It was kind of like

30

they were someone else's, someone J.D. didn't even know. But I nodded in understanding, being careful not to betray my thoughts.

"And the prognosis?" I quizzed.

He shrugged again. "I'll survive. But all of the clothes I was wearing have already gone to the incinerator."

"Clothes can be replaced," I reminded.

"So can I." I had no idea how to respond to that and stared silently while he said, "The Bauers could replace me, and Keenan could; and no one else would have to."

"I'm sorry…" I said, finally. "I don't understand…"

He looked at me, suddenly, as if realizing for the first time I was in the room with him. "Sorry. Never mind, it's nothing. Thoughts swallowed; catharsis aborted." Then he gave me a smile that didn't quite light up those deep, blue eyes.

"J.D.-" I began.

He cut me off. "I'm okay, Aine. Just forget about it, all right?"

"Okay," I said, slowly. "So, how are you enjoying your stay?" Yeah, that was lame; way to go, Annie.

"Not bad, actually. The food is terrible, but I get to sleep a lot. I like sleep."

"I bet I could help you with the food," I told him.

"Really?"

"Yeah. Do you like junk food?" Like you have to ask a teenage boy that question.

He laughed. "That's only thing I ever buy. Whenever I get money, I spend it on potato chips, candy, and spearmint gum."

"Pop?"

"Coke's my favorite."

"Okay. If you hang on for a few minutes, I'll be right back."

"Well, I don't have any money now."

"It's a gift."

"No, not after you saved my life. I can't repay-"

"That isn't the point, J.D." I explained as I left. I was able to purchase all of J.D.'s choices from a vending machine. J.D. accepted the snacks, smiling and thanking me like no one had ever done anything nice for him before.

"Do you want some?" he asked as he opened the candy.

"No, thanks. I had a good lunch today - something you don't get when you're a patient in a hospital."

J.D. nodded in agreement as he chewed on a handful of Reese's Pieces.

"What have they got you on in here?"

"Glucose and Tylenol - without codeine this time. Nothing hard."

"How's the pain?"

"I can deal with it." He tilted his head back, tossed the rest of the candy in his mouth, and reached for the chips.

"Do you know when you'll be released?"

He shrugged.

"Any idea?"

"Not really," he responded around a mouthful of chips.

"That's gross, J.D."

He swallowed hard and said, "Sorry." He popped a few more chips into his mouth.

"You seem to be doing well."

He shrugged yet again, finished the chips, and gulped his Coke. He swallowed again and looked at me, linking his blue eyes with my green ones. "Where do you live, Dr. Aine?"

His eyes held me, and I didn't even hesitate for half a second before telling this virtual stranger – meaning good or ill – exactly where to find me. "In Northwood on Hickory."

"Wow. Nice place. Of course, you do go to Lincoln."

"Where do you live?" I asked him.

He laughed, in a sardonic tone, and shrugged again. "Here."

"Where do you go to school?"

"Ford."

The average student at Ford was lower middle class. No "Junior Retreat" at that place...but no asbestos either (it was apparently all-the-rage when Port Morgan's schools were last remodeled, and Ford hadn't sprung for it).

"Got any brothers or sisters?" he asked me then.

"Two brothers and a sister, all younger. You?"

He shrugged. "Your parents still together?"

I raised my eyebrows. That was an odd question, not one a person would usually ask someone they'd known for barely a day. "Yeah," I answered. "They've been married over eighteen years. Yours?"

He shrugged. Again. I was beginning to wonder if this kid even knew who he was. I watched as he finished his Coke and started to un-wrap a piece of gum. "Mmmm…" he said, as he popped the fluorescent, green/yellow strip into his mouth. "I haven't eaten this well in years."

I laughed. "I'm sure you haven't."

"Seriously though, thanks."

"You're welcome. Again."

"And thanks for coming. I like sleep, but twenty-two hours a day is pretty much my limit."

"Thank you for letting me stay. I'm having fun."

He shook his head in disbelief. "You're weird."

"I know. So are you."

"Yeah, but I have an excuse."

"And what's that?"

He shrugged once more. I searched his face, and our eyes locked for a few seconds before he looked away. His gaze fell on my card which was sitting in his lap, and he picked it up and gripped it in his good hand. He was still holding it when my dad, wearing green scrubs and a white lab coat, popped his head into the room a couple minutes later.

"*Alannah*," Dad told me, "the patient needs his rest. Say goodbye." You may not know this, but "the patient needs his rest" can also be code for "go home and do your homework."

I frowned and stood up. "I guess visiting hours are over," I said.

J.D. nodded and asked me a question that surprised me even more than the one about my parents' relationship. He nodded at the doorway. "So your dad's a doctor?" he said, in a tone that was more of a statement. I was surprised because I doubted my dad was treating J.D., and Dad would have no reason to explain our relationship even if he was.

"What makes you think that's my dad?" I asked.

"Well, I didn't think your priest would be moonlighting in the medical field."

"Somebody told you he was my father?"

"He called you *alannah*."

"You speak Gaelic?"

"No. That isn't English?"

"No. How do you know what it means?"

"I don't know."

Neither of us spoke for a minute before I said, "Well, I guess I'd better go. I'll see you tomorrow?"

He looked up at me. "You'll come tomorrow?"

"Sure. If you'll have me."

"Of course. That's cool."

"Bye." I offered my hand again for him to shake, and while he seemed not to notice it, I knew that he had. Instead of making a deal out of it, I put it in my jacket pocket.

"Bye, Aine," J.D. said as I headed out the door.

*****

When Dad got home from work that evening, he came to my room to say hello. "So," he asked. "How'd your visit with the boyo go?" I faltered when he asked that. My Dad only uses "boyo" as a term of endearment for my brothers or, reflexively, in reference to a boy about whom he's deeply concerned. I wondered if my dad had heard something bad about J.D.'s condition.

"Um, fine," I said. "It was a little odd." Or J.D. was a little odd; okay, quite possibly the oddest person I'd ever met - in my entire life. It had been a strange conversation.

"Yeah?" Dad asked, waiting for me to elaborate.

"J.D.'s...well, strange. He's an interesting person; seems intelligent, good sense of humor, all that. But it also seems he'd like me to believe that he lives in the hospital, doesn't know a thing about his parents' relationship; doesn't know if he has any siblings or not, doesn't even know his age exactly or his first name."

My father sighed deeply, and I asked, "What?"

"Well, as it seems, he's being honest with you about all of that."

"Huh? Does he have amnesia?"

He frowned and said, "No, but just over fourteen years ago, J.D. was found living alone in an alley in Lansing. He was questioned by police and social workers, but the only pertinent information he could offer about himself was that sometimes he was called 'J.D.' and sometimes he was called 'Dillon.' So he was designated, 'Jay Dillon Foster'. They figured he was about three years old and designated the day he was found as his third birthday, but they had no way of knowing."

I frowned. J.D. didn't have a first name, and his last name wasn't actually his and was, considering how he'd gotten it, only slightly less corny than Doe or Public. The state had ended up with a kid who had no family, no birthday, no name, no identity, just a vague description about blond hair, blue eyes, and a speech impediment. J.D. didn't know who he was.

"J.D.'s been in a couple bad homes," my dad was saying. "The man he lived with from the time he was about four-and-a-half until he was nine was put in prison and later murdered by an inmate because of things he did to J.D. It was bad enough that even though the guy was in prison, they moved J.D. to a new county for his own safety. After all that, he was too 'damaged' for most of the other families he lived with to justify a serious effort to help him. He first went to live with a contractor and wife named Bauer when he was thirteen. Since then, J.D.'s run away three times and visited the E.R. nine times for 'work-related' injuries."

I nodded understanding. "Injures that weren't truly 'work-related,' huh?" I asked.

"The police could never prove anything. Yesterday, Mr. Bauer took J.D. into your school about 3:00 a.m. so they could work on installing the insulation in the fine arts building. In that building, the space between the ceiling and the roof used to be a bona fide attic, and Bauer decided since the room was available, it would be easier to work from up in the attic than try to hoist the insulation in through the bottom. They'd set up a workstation in the loft behind the stage in the auditorium and created walkways by laying sheets of plywood over the rafters. About six-thirty, they were just starting on the choir room, and J.D. was tired; he'd gotten up at two o'clock after working late the night before. J.D. sat down on a workbench to rest, and Bauer shouted at him to get back to work. J.D. complained he hadn't taken any 'uppers' like Bauer had, and Bauer nailed him above the eye with a scrap of wood. The blow dazed J.D. and gave

Bauer a chance to fracture his rib, break his finger, cover his entire body in bruises…"

My father's voice trailed away, and he took a deep breath before going on. "Bauer didn't want an audience when he took the boyo out of the building; and with all the teachers and students beginning to arrive, that was a big concern. He forced several Tylenol 3 pills down J.D.'s throat and waited for him to start falling asleep, at which point, he took him down the walkway over the choir room and left him lying on a piece of plywood, taking down the boards that led back to the loft. Bauer probably exited the building through the auditorium about 7:50, just as the choir was beginning to arrive in its classroom. At 8:20, the plywood shifted and dropped J.D. through the ceiling."

"How'd you find all that out?" I asked my dad.

"J.D.'s arrival made a pretty big stir at the hospital. The police, news reporters, and Ms. Keenan were all over the place, talking and asking questions." The presence of reporters meant that the weekly was publishing J.D.'s story in the next issue.

"Who is Ms. Keenan?" I asked.

"A caseworker for the Family Independence Agency."

"I asked J.D. if she was his mother." I groaned. "He doesn't have a mother."

Dad sat beside me and pulled me into his arms. "Annie, you didn't know."

I remembered the bag of clothes in the wardrobe; that was probably everything he owned. "He doesn't have a home now. He doesn't know when he's getting out of the hospital, 'cause he's got no place to go."

"Well, it's good he doesn't have to go back to the Bauers'. If he'd stayed with them, they would've killed him eventually."

"But where will he go?"

"I don't know."

I felt the tears come.

"Why don't we pray?" he said.

Chapter five-

Prayers are always answered. This one got a yes.

When I went to see J.D. on Wednesday, I brought more food, a stuffed lizard, a quarter pound of gourmet chocolates, and Mark and Shannon, both with cards. J.D. did vaguely remember Mark from the choir room and could tell right off that Shannon was my little sister from our shared auburn hair, green eyes, and freckled, ivory skin. J.D. seemed to like Shannon quite a bit, and I thought that was cool. He still didn't shake any of our hands, dodging contact in ways that seemed increasingly lame to me; I started to wonder about that.

At church that night, as Shannon and I were walking into the building, we met Jim and Karen Jacobs. The Jacobs live in the Northwood neighborhood, about half a mile from my family. They have four daughters who have all graduated from Lincoln, and Mr. Jacobs is on Lincoln's school board. Mr. and Mrs. Jacobs' fourth granddaughter was just born over Thanksgiving break. When they saw Shannon and me, they greeted us, and Mrs. Jacobs said, "Mrs.

Greene told me that you're quite the hero, Annie." (Explanation: Mrs. Greene is Lincoln's choir director.)

I flushed at her comment and shrugged, "None of his injuries were critical, anyway."

"But you did great. How is the young man? What's his name?" Mr. Jacobs asked.

"J.D. He's well, just cuts and bruises mostly. We just came from visiting him."

"That's nice," Mrs. Jacobs said.

Mr. Jacobs asked, "Did they find out who did that to him?"

"Yeah. It was his foster father."

"That's terrible," Mrs. Jacobs responded. "We've taken in a few foster children over the years. I can't imagine how a person could do that to a child, especially one who's already hurting so much."

"It's pretty sick," I agreed.

"Have they found him a new place to live?"

"Not yet."

"That's terrible. After all he's been through, he's homeless, too."

"Sure'n you could have him if you wanted him," Shannon blurted in her cute imitation of a stage Irish accent.

"Shannon!" I admonished, feeling the pale skin on my cheeks and neck going hot pink.

Mr. and Mrs. Jacobs smiled as if to say, "And isn't she just the cutest?"

Three days later J.D. was moving in with the Jacobses.

All of J.D.'s earthly possessions fit into his duffel bag and two packing boxes that been quartered underneath Keenan's desk at FIA for the duration of his hospital stay. Though unpacking the items into J.D's new room required a minimal investment of time, both Mark and I showed up to "help."

Mark sat at the foot of J.D.'s bed sipping pop from a can while I pulled items one by one from the boxes and asked J.D. where each should be placed. J.D. answered each question absently, while he folded and refolded each item of clothing that he then shoved unceremoniously into the top drawer of the dresser. Mark and I regarded J.D.'s process with curiosity, noting that his carelessness in putting the clothes in the drawer undid all the work he invested in the folding itself. After several glances in J.D.'s direction, Mark and I looked at each other and shrugged.

"Where do you want this?" I asked J.D., holding up a worn paperback copy of Ray Bradbury's *Something Wicked This Way Comes*.

He rolled his eyes and gestured vaguely at the small, nearly empty bookshelf next to his closet. I set the Bradbury next to a hardback reprint of *A Christmas Carol* that the Jacobses had placed in the room. I returned to the box; pulled out a baseball (dated 1989, but well-preserved), and held it up for J.D. to see. "What about this?"

He glanced at the ball before looking back at the t-shirt he was folding for the third time. "I don't care," he told me.

"Does it have any sentimental significance?"

"No."

"It looks like you took good care of it. Thought maybe you got it at a game or something."

"Like I've ever been to a baseball game?" His voice was incredulous. "It came in a used grocery bag from a foster kid charity organization. There was also a package of crackers, and I did not cry over the loss when I ate them."

I nodded and set the baseball in the drawer next to his clothes. He glanced at it for a second before picking it up and tossing it into his closet. I watched him fold the t-shirt a fourth time before I chose the next item from the box.

The object was a 4x6 picture frame, but the picture inside had been turned so all that was visible was the gray "Kodak" imprint on the back. Wanting to fix this oversight, I turned the frame over, flipped back the catches, and pulled the back panel out. The back panel was stubborn at first then popped out suddenly, and four 4x6 photos and a dozen wallet-sized portraits fell from the frame onto the floor. I sat down, turned the photos all face-up, and lined them up in rows. The wallet-sized photos were school "Picture Day" prints of a boy I recognized as J.D. The 4x6's reminded me of full-face police mug-shots. I picked up one of a three-year-old J.D. that must have been taken shortly after he'd been found. He'd been a cute kid.

"What's that?" Mark asked me, leaning forward to see what I had in my hands.

J.D. glanced at me then and did a double take. "What are you doing?" he asked, sounding ticked. He knelt and grabbed up the photos in one sweep, leaving only his Kindergarten and fifth grade photos behind. He snatched the frame and shoved the photos back into it so none of the faces were visible. I pocketed the two photos he'd left behind and showed him the one I was already holding. "Where'd you get the ones like this?" I asked.

"My first social worker gave them to me when she retired," he said. He reached for the photo, but I held it out of his reach.

"When was that?"

"That was right after I-...I was like nine."

"You were a cute kid."

"Oh." He turned, shoved the picture frame into the empty bottom drawer of his dresser, and grabbed an old pair of jeans to fold.

"May I borrow these? I bet I could scan them and print pretty nice copies."

"Why would you want to?"

45

"They'd be nice to have. They're adorable."

"Do whatever you want," he said as he folded his jeans for the fourth time before shaking them out and starting again. "I don't care."

It was then I understood J.D.'s folding technique was more to distract himself from everything else than organize his dresser. The gathering to get him settled had turned into a "stroll down memory lane" for J.D., a re-visitation of memories he would've rather forgotten.

*****

The next Friday, J.D. was dropping himself on the carpeting in my parents' living room while Mark, Ben, Juli, and I listened to his description of life with his new family. "I didn't mind her getting me these," he was saying as he slapped the knees of his new, khaki zip-offs. "'Cause these are practical. Two-in-one. I got pants; and, when summer comes, I'll have shorts, too."

"Well, that's a pretty nice shirt too," I said, referring to the greenish/khaki-colored t-shirt he was wearing.

"Yeah, well, everything she's gotten me is nice," J.D. agreed, "but I don't want her to think that she has to buy me stuff."

"She knows she doesn't have to," Juli told him.

"She wants to," Ben added.

"Yeah, it's what-" Juli started.

"-Parents do. Besides," Ben continued, "It's not like they're getting you anything-"

"-that they can't afford." (Yeah, Ben and Juli have been together for almost two years, and sometimes they finish each other's sentences; it's, like, too cute.)

"They sure are doing the parent thing," Mark commented.

J.D. groaned, but the noise had a happy tone to it. "Yesterday, when Jim got home from work, he dragged me outside to throw a baseball. Back and forth, back and forth. It was strange."

Juli giggled at J.D.'s expression, and Mark said, "That is called 'playing catch,' J.D. It's a very popular father-son pastime."

"You'll have to humor him," I told J.D. "He's spent the last twenty-eight years raising four daughters. Their three temporary foster kids were all girls, and now they have four granddaughters. Having you around is probably really cool for him."

"I'm not really their kid."

"Don't tell them that," Juli said. "They'd be shocked and very upset."

"Nobody wants state kids, Juliana. We're just here."

"J.D.," I said, "if they didn't want you, you wouldn't be living in their house."

"I've been in a lot of places where I wasn't wanted, Annie."

"Jim and Karen are different."

He sighed and wrapped his arms around his legs. Nobody said anything for a while, and J.D. finally stood up. "I gotta get back," he said. "The younger two Jacobs girls are coming over tonight to meet me."

"Want a ride?" I asked.

"I'll be fine."

"Half a mile can be a long, cold walk in the dark in Michigan in early December, J.D."

"Well, okay."

I told Mark, Juli, and Ben that I'd be back in a few minutes, and J.D. and I left. Since J.D. had found out the Jacobses lived so close to my family, he spent many of his waking hours with us. He'd even helped Mom shovel the driveway while my siblings and I were in school.

"Jim and Karen are pretty cool though," J.D. told me as we climbed into my six-year-old Honda Accord and started off. "Hands down the best family that I've been in - since I could remember, I mean. They said if the shoe store where I applied hired me; or, if any place hired me, I'd get to keep the money I made. I've never had more money than I could get from returning bottles or finding change."

"That'll be cool, then."

J.D. nodded and was silent for a while.

"But you're depressed about something?" I asked, finally.

"Well, they told me that Monday is going to be 'the Day'."

I understood his mood immediately. By "the Day," J.D. meant that was when he'd be starting back at school - not at Ford, at Lincoln. He wasn't excited about that at all. I felt bad for him. I mean, I had enough trouble getting along at Lincoln; I had no idea how he was going to do. "Mark, Ben, Juli, and I will be at Lincoln. Not all Lincoln kids are snots."

He looked at me and smiled but didn't seem altogether cheered-up.

"It'll be okay," I told him.

He didn't respond.

"So," I said as we pulled up to the Jacobs house. "I'll see you tomorrow?"

"You don't mind if I come over?"

"Not at all. Traditionally, people like having their friends around."

He smiled briefly before becoming serious. "Yeah, but I don't wanna overstay my welcome."

"You're not."

"But, if you ever want me to get lost, just tell me; and I'll go. Okay?"

"Whatever."

"Promise me."

"Fine. I promise."

"And you'll help me, like if I'm doing something wrong... bad manners or something, you'll tell me."

"Sure."

"Thanks. I'll see ya."

"Yeah. See ya."

J.D. hopped out of the car and ran to the house; I watched him go, feeling kind of sad. He was terrified all the time of being a burden; but at the same time, he was desperate for friendship.

Plus, I was picking up on something else...All that time he'd been hanging around or I would visit him, and I'd never seen him hug someone, shake anyone's hand, or even bump into someone accidentally. He never initiated any sort of physical contact with anyone. He always sat or stood where he had, at the very least, a foot of personal space in all directions. He actually flinched whenever someone came in contact with him, whether accidentally or on purpose. It almost looked like he was allergic to physical contact.

Whatever caused this strange behavior, it must've made him feel terribly isolated. And I wasn't sure I liked the way it broke my heart when he hurt.

Chapter six-

When J.D. started school at Lincoln, he had two classes with me, third hour social studies and sixth hour study hall. By third hour, he was stressed; by study hall, he was having a breakdown of what was left of his sanity. J.D. didn't talk to me; he simply made his appearance and asked for a library pass. I figured he wasn't planning on coming back, so I got a library pass of my own and went to find him. I checked the library first to make sure I'd understood what he'd been trying to pull. I had. I checked an empty classroom, the lecture room, and the auditorium, and I eventually found him in the loft of the auditorium…where he'd been attacked two weeks before. He was in a corner, with his knees pulled up to his chest and arms around his legs, staring off into space. "Aw, J.D.," I said, "why'd you come back here?"

His head turned towards me, but his eyes were blank.

"Hey, Jay Dillon," I called.

His eyebrows rose in a question, and his eyes focused on me slowly.

I walked over and sat down facing him. "Can I…" I faltered, "um…get you anything?"

"Get me anything?" he asked in surprise. A sardonic laugh jerked out of his throat. "How about life, death, and a fifth of whiskey to drown my sorrows?"

I frowned. "Life and death?"

"I've got to be alive before I'll be allowed to die, you know."

I didn't respond. I didn't know how to respond.

"You can't, right? The whiskey, then. I'm sure your parents have a liquor cabinet."

"J.D.-"

"No?" he interrupted. "Thanks, anyway. Have a nice life."

"I'm not going, anywhere," I told him. "Just tell me what's wrong."

"Well, first of all, apparently, I do have a real name, now. I have officially been christened 'Kid Who Fell Through the Ceiling.' Quite a mouthful, huh?"

"I'm sorry, J.D., but, you know, high school popularity aside, the average in-crowd kid at Lincoln is a social idiot."

He smiled slightly. "Sure'n that's the truth."

I giggled and shook my head. "Second of all, you're starting to talk like my little sister."

He gave a small snort/laugh. "And when did that happen, huh?"

"I don't know."

He sighed, and his barely-there smile disappeared, taking mine with it. "We laugh now, but what happens when they start beating on me?"

"J.D., I'm not advocating violence, but you have a right to defend yourself. Anyone can tell by looking at you that you're no wimp." I had a suspicion that J.D. knew how to handle physical conflict. You don't get knocked around for years without learning how to get away…or how to fight back.

"Sure," J.D. responded. "But any fight I get in will be all-my-fault, just because of who I am. I can't do that to Jim and Karen. Not after everything they've done to try to help."

"We'll pray it doesn't get to that."

J.D. didn't respond and started to zone-out again. I finally asked if anything else was bothering him. He raised his eyebrows, thought for a moment, and nodded slowly.

"Something with school?" I asked.

"No."

"Jim and Karen?"

He sighed and said, "They wanna buy me a car."

I swallowed my surprise and managed to say in an almost even tone that hid most of my confusion, "If they want to get it, why don't you want it?" I wanted to say, "Are you crazy?? Most kids

53

would kill if they thought it would get their parents to buy them a car."

"They feed me, let me live in their house, buy me clothes, a skateboard, CD's... They decorated an entire room in their house for me. How can I let them buy me a car?"

"J.D., it'll make them happy."

"But what if this doesn't work out? Then they've spent all of this money on stuff they can't use, and they'll hate me more because of it."

"Don't even think that, okay? It's not worth considering. It will work out. The Jacobses care about you too much to let it not work out. And, you know what? I don't think that you're willing to let this fall apart, either."

He sighed and shrugged.

"It's true," I confirmed. I searched his face for a moment. He didn't exactly grin, but I saw a little bit of something lift from his face, like a tiny bit of the cloud over him was blowing away. I forced a little bit of a smile before asking, "Want a hug?"

"No," he said, quickly before adding, as an afterthought. "That's okay, I mean. I'm fine."

He thought I'd be hurt by his rejection of the gesture, but I wasn't. I'd already known he wouldn't want me to touch him. "We should get back to class," I said

*****

J.D. almost could have been popular at Lincoln. Almost. On the surface, he seemed to have everything going for him. He had all the little things down great. The clothes Mrs. Jacobs had gotten him were good. Even though not everyone would've considered Jim and Karen Jacobs his real parents, they had enough money. He was intelligent; he didn't have any heritage to be embarrassed of; he was (forgive me) drop-dead gorgeous (and he didn't know it, which gave him a certain charm). And, as far as the Deciding Factor, he was athletic. Very much so. He liked skateboarding and street hockey a lot, and he had enough basketball skill that he could've made a starting spot on the school team.

Two things got in the way of any ambitions for popularity he may or may not have had. The first was that he didn't participate in any school sports, so no one outside our group of friends ever saw his athletic ability. I'd spent a lot of time in consideration over exactly why he didn't participate in school sports, and I'd decided the most logical reason was the team camaraderie that's present at Lincoln. Our teams are always punching each other, patting each other's shoulders, high-fiving each other, and slapping each other's... Right. Well, if anyone had tried to do any of that to J.D., I expect they'd have found themselves on the way to the hospital for emergency limb reattachment.

The second was that Lincoln had one more very important popularity rule. In order to be a member of Lincoln High's ruling social party, one should never, under any circumstances, "make a scene." It was okay to be severely confused or even emotionally demented, as long as it stayed hidden. In order to be in Lincoln's in-crowd, you weren't allowed to draw any attention to yourself in a manner considered by them to be "bad." J.D. violated that rule on his second day at Lincoln, during third hour.

My social studies teacher has this thing he does where he'll assign class work and then patrol the room and watch us do it, as if we were kindergartners; and while he is standing behind us staring at our work, he'll put a hand on our shoulder (Can you see where this is heading?).

That Tuesday, we were working on some class work when I glanced over at J.D. in the seat catty-corner, to the right and front, of my own, and saw the teacher heading toward him. Before I could think of anything to do, the teacher arrived behind J.D.'s desk, and the hand landed on J.D.'s shoulder. J.D. scrambled out of his seat and away from the hand, sending his desk flying a few feet. He turned to face the teacher and backed away until he was satisfied with the space between them.

"Mr. Foster," said the stunned teacher, standing in the spot where J.D.'s desk should've been. "Take your seat and complete the assignment."

"No," J.D. responded.

"Mr. Foster, I will not allow you to continue disrupting my class." Hand outstretched, he took a step toward J.D., and J.D. backed away again, almost tripping over a stack of books that another student had left in the aisle.

"Mr. Foster! Come here, pick up your desk, and sit down."

J.D. shook his head vigorously in the manner of a frightened, yet contrary child.

"What is *wrong* with you?" the teacher asked, making a sharp gesture at J.D. J.D. flinched, lifting his arm to protect his face in the same gesture he had used when he was unconscious, and I'd tried to clean the cut above his eye. The teacher was shaken up and gave J.D. an odd, confused look before regaining his authoritative demeanor. "Go to the vice principal's office, Mr. Foster."

J.D. left the room relieved, and he didn't get in trouble over the incident, not with the administration at least. The vice principal arranged to shuffle his schedule; J.D. landed in Mark's AP social studies class, Ben and Juli's English class, and my French class. Then Keenan conducted a special conference about him with his new teachers.

A major scene was made, but it has since become a joke with us. J.D. likes to say he wasn't popular in high school because of his speech impediment.

Chapter seven –

On the Saturday after J.D. started school, he drove his new car – a used Saturn – into our driveway. He stepped out and announced that he had figured out why Jim and Karen had wanted to get him a car: so they'd have something to take away when he got in trouble. I shook my head, and Shannon and I hopped into the car for a run down the highway. We got back to the house about five, just as Mom was getting home from a craft class she taught at the community center. Mom set J.D. and me up in the living room with hot chocolate and Christmas cookies.

"How do you think your first week at Lincoln went?" I asked J.D.

He was chewing on a cookie and simply rolled his eyes incredulously in response.

"Well, now you get two weeks off to recover."

He nodded and gulped down half of his hot chocolate before getting up to look at our Christmas tree. "You have candy on your tree?" he asked, fingering one of the rainbow-colored cherry candy canes.

"Yeah," I said, surprised at the question. I'd found that J.D. wasn't quite familiar with Christmas traditions. When he'd gotten his first sight of our freshly-cut and decorated Christmas tree, he'd asked completely seriously, "Why do you have a tree in your living room?"

After an extended explanation that took a lot longer than it should have because it took me a long time to figure out where to start, he told me that he had seen Christmas trees in malls and stuff but hadn't realized people put them in their homes. It had shocked me, but I'd figured that maybe it wasn't impossible to live seventeen years without a Christmas tree. The Bauers had never celebrated holidays with him, and the guy who'd been put in prison had held J.D. in a pretty much dungeon-like life. He'd lived with a Jewish family for a few years, and he hadn't been anywhere else for more than a few months. He'd never watched much television either, so the *Charlie Brown Christmas Special* hadn't been part of his upbringing.

"You can have one if you want," I told him, nodding at a candy cane. "Those are cherry. Take a peppermint one, too."

He eagerly took two candy canes off the tree. I watched as he un-wrapped the peppermint one, broke off a small piece of it, and popped it into his mouth.

"Don't the Jacobses have candy canes on their tree?"

He shrugged, his favorite form of communication. "They said they put their tree up on Christmas Eve."

"Some people do that."

"Do you know their daughters?"

"Sure. I know the younger ones better, but I've been to church with all of them."

"I've met Theresa and Daria; they're the ones still in college."

"Yeah. The others are Lisa and Sarah."

"Do you know their families?"

"Sure. Lisa is married to Eric; they have Maya, Lily, and Teia. Sarah is married to Kieran, and they have baby Shelby."

"They're all coming on the 23rd and staying through Christmas morning. Wanna come over before they get here and show me who's who in family pictures?" He paused to slurp on the piece of candy cane in his mouth and went back to examining the trappings on my family's Christmas tree. "So I know who they are, I mean."

"Sure."

"I appreciate that."

"No problem. Tell me what else is going on for Christmas."

"They bought me a...uh, big sock?"

"A stocking?" I asked.

"That's it. They took me to a card store and had me pick out an ornament of my own to put on the tree. They asked me what kind of dinner I wanted for Christmas Eve. I said pizza, and that's what we're going to eat."

It was fun watching J.D. talk about Christmas. All the traditions I'd known all my life, J.D. was experiencing for the first time. His fascination with these things was similar to Shannon's. It injected some of the child-like magic back into my Christmas, him being so stoked about his own. "They asked me what I wanted for Christmas! Do you believe that? They just bought me a car."

"What did you ask for?"

"A CD and a couple of books."

"And what did they say?"

"'Don't you want anything else?'"

I smiled.

"I told them just to keep feeding me," J.D. continued. Which could be difficult enough, I thought. J.D.'s stomach was a veritable black hole. He'd been at my house for fifteen minutes, and he'd eaten an apple, leftover macaroni, nine cookies, six jumbo marshmallows, and a candy cane. "And they said, 'Seriously, though.' So I asked for a hockey stick, a street hockey puck, and blue Chuck Taylors, thinking I was being silly. They said, 'Good. Anything else?'" I watched his face break into a smile. "I've decided I like Christmas," he announced.

"So you're coming to grips with their spending money on you?" I asked.

"I guess. It seems to make them happy, so…" He shrugged. "Yeah."

"Normally, that wouldn't make me feel good about someone buying me a lot of stuff, but I feel like they're doing it because they want to take care of me."

"They just want to be sure you have everything you need and a few things you want, too."

"And they aren't just spending money on me; they're spending time with me, playing catch and talking about school. They're teaching me things, like how to change the oil in my car and make an omelet." He looked at me for a second before turning back to the tree and fingering an ornament. "You know," he said suddenly, "I think they really do want me."

"Of course they do."

He grinned and gave a soft laugh. "I've got a family. Imagine that." He glanced at the tree for a moment more before coming to sit beside me. He took two cookies off the plate on the coffee table and handed one to me. I took a bite.

"Hey, guys." It was Ben. We looked up to see that he, Mark, and Juliana had arrived for movie night. I swallowed the cookie and said hello.

"Your mom sent popcorn," Juliana stated, balancing the bowl on J.D.'s knees. Like me, Juliana finds J.D.'s eating habits humorous. He'll never ask for food, but he'll eat anything that's put in front of him (I do mean anything). We knew teenaged boys could eat a lot, but J.D.'s appetite seemed even to exceed that. She and I exchanged a look as he immediately dug in and shoved an entire handful of popcorn into his mouth.

He saw the look and said, "What?" around a mouthful of popcorn.

"J.D., that's gross," I said.

He snapped his mouth shut, looking sheepish.

*****

On the 23rd, I went to the Jacobs house to go through photos with J.D., and he could recognize everyone by the time they arrived. True to form, he didn't shake any hands or give any hugs, but the family didn't seem to expect it. I suspect Mr. and Mrs. Jacobs had already discussed that with their daughters.

J.D. seemed to like the family, but was especially intrigued by little Shelby. Sarah had set Shelby in her car seat down on the living room floor, and J.D. noticed her while he was walking by. First, he stopped and watched her curiously. I realized it was possible he'd never seen a person as small as Shelby. Then she started whimpering, and J.D. sat down in front of her and began rocking her seat and making faces at her. I sat down with him to watch. He'd been entertaining her for a few minutes when Sarah noticed. "Do you want to hold her?" she asked him. "You're welcome to pick her up."

"No," J.D. told her. "That's all right."

"I don't mind."

J.D. shrugged and shook his head.

"If you ever do, go ahead. All right?"

"All right."

Sarah walked away, and J.D. went back to rocking and making faces, being careful not to touch even that tiny child. But I took it as a good sign that he had gotten closer to her than he had anyone else.

Chapter eight-

J.D. came to my house just after 3:00 p.m. on Christmas Day. I met him at the side door to hang up his coat, and my cousin Ingrid, who's about a year younger than me, followed me. "Hey, Jay Dillon," I greeted. "What's up?"

"Hey, Aine. Do you want me to leave? Am I interrupting something?"

"No, you're fine. It's good to see you. By the way, Merry Christmas."

"Same to you."

"Did everyone leave then?" I quizzed.

"Right before I did."

I almost asked him if I could get him anything, but then I remembered what he'd said the last time I'd asked him that, and I wasn't able to get the question out of my mouth. I stood staring dumbly into those deep, blue eyes of his. He returned my gaze for a moment before his eyes widened in an oh-right expression.

"Hey," he said. "Look." He pointed down at his feet, and I saw a brand-new pair of Converse Chuck Taylors.

"Nice," I said.

"Can you believe they got them? Well, probably you can, but I'm surprised." I smiled. He watched me for a moment then suddenly blurted, "They got me a Bible."

"Well, good," I responded.

"One of my own," he went on. "A nice one. Leather cover and…notes and stuff."

"Study aids?"

"Yeah. Why did they get it?"

"They were probably hoping you'd read it."

He hit his left palm against his forehead in a "duh" gesture.

"Will you?" I asked.

He shrugged and looked down at his feet. I glanced at my cousin. "Hey, J.D.," I said, and he looked back up at me. "This is my cousin, Ingrid. Ingrid, J.D."

"Hi," J.D. greeted mildly, studying her.

"Hello, J.D.," my cousin said in a slightly flirtatious manner. "It's great to meet you." She offered her hand to be shaken (or kissed, I never could tell because of how she did it). J.D. pretended not to notice her hand, but at the same time shoved his own hands into the pockets of his hoodie to make it clear he had no intention of shaking (or kissing) hers. Ingrid got this annoyed, offended look that she gets sometimes and made a show of taking back her hand. I tried to ignore her and asked J.D. if he'd like to come meet some more of my family. Ingrid recovered quickly as we moved out of the entryway. "Is J.D. a nickname?" she asked him.

"Yes," he told her.

Duh, I thought.

"Some people call me 'Edie'," Ingrid told him.

"Oh."

"Where are you from?"

"Half a mile from here."

"Really? That's nice." She grabbed his wrist, and he yanked it away. I watched, noticing a bright pink flush around his wrist and wondering how tight she'd grabbed him. He moved away from her and closer to me, and she got offended again.

Walking through the dining room, I grabbed a plate of about a dozen homemade cookies and candies. I absently handed it to J.D., and he offered some to both Ingrid and me. We declined, and he popped a piece of chocolate-covered toffee into his mouth. We went to the living room, and I introduced J.D. to my aunts, my uncle, and the rest of my cousins. Then the three of us and T.J. went down to the rec room in the basement to hang out. J.D. offered T.J. some of the cookies on the plate (he'd already finished up all of the candy). T.J. declined; and J.D. popped back a chocolate chip cookie. He finished that and ate a wreath cookie before asking Ingrid where she was from. He used that tone people have when they aren't interested in the answer but thought it would be impolite not to ask, since they'd been asked the same question.

"Well," she began as she scooted closer to him. He scooted away and started in on another cookie. "I live in Schaumberg," she informed him. "Do you know where that is?"

"Sure," he said. "In Illinois. It's a suburb of Chicago. I was living in Chicago this summer."

"Why?" T.J. asked him.

"That was the third time I left the Bauers. I wanted to be far away."

"Where's Bauers?" Ingrid questioned.

"They were my foster parents."

"Why'd you run away?"

"I got sick of being beat up on."

T.J. asked, "Why didn't you just tell your social worker what they were doing?"

J.D. finished the last cookie, shrugged, and said, with deep and complete graveness, "Keenan is a sick, evil being."

We were all stunned at J.D.'s statement, and Ingrid asked, "Why would you say that?"

J.D. didn't respond but stood suddenly saying, "I should get back. Jim and Karen will want me to spend some time with them." He looked at me. "Go figure, huh?" His tone was light-hearted, but his blue eyes held pain I couldn't imagine. My heart broke.

After J.D. was gone, Ingrid and I settled in my room to play cards. "Man, what rock did you find that one under, Annie?" Ingrid asked me once we were alone.

I sighed and tried my best to keep my temper under control.

Ingrid went on. "I didn't think you'd ever become superficial, Annie. Then I meet him. I'm really disappointed in you. You've disillusioned me. He's cute, but that's all he's got going for him. He seems a little light in the intelligence area, and he's rude and arrogant, wouldn't even condescend to shake my hand."

I put up with a lot before I spoke up. "Stop, Ingrid," I said. "You don't know J.D., and you don't understand. He doesn't shake anybody's hand, not even mine, not even his foster parents'."

"Yeah, well, at least he didn't brush you off like a bug."

"I didn't grab him."

"That shouldn't matter. What kind of person can't stand to touch another?"

"You don't understand what happened to him."

"That doesn't make sense, and even if it did, he's still a glutton."

"What do you mean?"

"Didn't you see how he was with those cookies? He wasn't hungry, but he ate them all."

"Okay, Ingrid, I want you to stop." But, looking back, I could see she was right about that last thing. He'd eaten that entire plate of treats when he hadn't wanted any of them. But he'd forced them down…just like he had the popcorn and the fruit and the marshmallows and the cookies that day he got his car, just like he always did. He ate like he might never get fed again. That was the first time I wondered if his odd eating habits, like the whole physical contact issue, might have a psychological basis.

Ingrid was still going. "I mean, it's revolting. He just-"

"Ingrid," I interrupted. "Shut up."

"Annie, if I were you, I'd leave him behind. He's like plastic food. All look, no substance. He hasn't even learned to pronounce his r's correctly, like any five-year-old."

I slapped her.

She stared at me for a full minute before blurting, "I'm telling my Mama."

"Go right ahead," I told her. I turned around and grabbed my coat.

"Where are you going?" she asked in her best "righteously indignant" voice.

"To see J.D."

"I'm disappointed in you, Annie."

"Just shut up, Ingrid."

When I got to the Jacobses' house, Karen told me J.D. wasn't feeling well and was resting in his room. I could've kicked myself for giving him all that junk. I normally wouldn't have gone up to his bedroom, but I needed to talk to him, so I went up, knocked lightly on the door, and let myself in when he didn't answer. I opened the door quietly, in case he was asleep; I wanted to talk to him, but I didn't want to wake him up to do it. He was curled up on his bed, on top of the blankets, with his back to the door. A can of 7-Up sat on his nightstand next to his new Bible and a new hardcover novel. "Hey, J.D." I called softly enough that I wouldn't wake him if he was asleep.

He turned over, looked at me, and smiled slightly. "Hey, Aine," he greeted.

"You all right?" I asked him.

"Got a stomachache," he told me.

"That's what I hear. Imagine: your first real Christmas, and I go and make you sick."

He slowly shifted himself into a sitting position and shrugged. "It's all right. You didn't ruin my day or anything." He picked up the 7-Up and took a sip before continuing. "Everyone seemed to like the cookies I decorated."

"You decorated cookies?"

"It was Karen's idea. I didn't have any money, and I told her the only thing I could do was draw pictures. She helped me make cookies yesterday, and I put pictures on them. I made some for you, but they were in my coat, and I forgot. Here."

He opened the top drawer of his nightstand, pulled out a rectangular food container, and handed it to me. I opened it and saw two square cookies that sported frosting cartoon pictures: one of the living room at my house and one of my locker at Lincoln, decked out for Christmas. "Like I said," he went on, "it was Karen's idea, and I couldn't come up with a better one. Everybody likes cookies."

"These are incredible, J.D. So you're an artist? That's cool."

He shrugged. "You really like 'em?"

"Yeah. I'm gonna have to take a picture before I eat them."

"Yeah, they taste good, too."

I smiled. "Thanks, J.D. These are a cool gift."

He grinned. "Merry Christmas."

"Same to you. My family sent some stuff that we forgot about when you were at the house." Shannon had made a card for him and enclosed a picture of the nativity that she'd drawn. Mark, Ben, Juliana, and I had all chipped in to buy him gift certificates for a local restaurant, and my parents had gotten him a digital wristwatch that showed military time. J.D. examined the gifts, smiled, and asked me to thank everyone for him.

"I'm glad you like them. I'm sure everyone else will be, too."

72

"This is a good Christmas, Aine, even though I'm not feeling great right now."

"It is, but about that…"

"Yeah?"

"J.D., if I give you food, and you're not hungry, or don't want it, it's all right to say no or ask if you can hang onto it until later. A lot of it's my fault, because I saw you'd eat anything and decided to feed you and feed you…to see if you'd explode or whatever; and it wasn't good judgment on my part. But I'm over it - it's fine to say no. Eat only what you want; and, well, the next meal is always gonna be just a few hours away."

J.D.'s face and neck suddenly flushed a hot red, before the last sentence was completely out of my mouth. He looked at me with a pained expression. "I can't help thinking this is gonna end…you know, one second everything will be fine, but the next it will be…over. I try to tell myself everything's fine, everything's great, but I can't help questioning that. It seems crazy on one hand, but on the other, it seems the sanest thing ever to be prepared. That's what's always happened before; I don't get why it shouldn't happen now."

"I can understand that, J.D. If I were looking at it from your perspective, I'd probably feel the same way. But I can also tell you my perspective, and Jim and Karen's perspective, and this time is different. You're here because God wants you here, and I know that

God wouldn't have dropped you down out of the ceiling and taken you this far if He was suddenly going to up and leave you without options. God doesn't leave a job unfinished; I know that without question."

"But how can you know that? Especially considering my situation with my parents. I'm probably just a mistake."

I frowned. "That doesn't matter. I know that beyond a shadow of a doubt. I also know that I am, as you so sweetly and eloquently put it, a mistake."

"No." He searched my face and saw I wasn't joking. "You?" he asked.

"I was so, totally *not* planned on. I had a father in medical school and a mother who was trying to work to put him through. I did not fit into their schedule at all. But here I am. And they love me so much I can see it in their eyes every time they look at me." Having finished my speech, I sat down hard on the floor beside the bed and gave a slightly put-on sigh of relief for emphasis. Even after that, however, he was still frowning, so I went on, "And, you know what, J.D.? People make mistakes, but God doesn't. If your biological parents thought you were a mistake and used that as justification to leave you, the problem was theirs, not yours. And that problem was the only real mistake."

"You're good, Annie, but…" He shook his head. "It's hard to believe that after everything that's happened. Especially when I know Keenan's still in control of me and everything else that-" His voice choked off, and he reached for the can of 7-Up.

"J.D.," I asked, "What's wrong with Keenan?"

"Everything. She's sick. She-" He stopped. "You don't wanna hear this."

"Yeah, I do."

"No, you don't understand, Aine. I can tell by the way you're saying it, like it's not a big deal. You haven't heard enough, seen enough to understand there are some things you would rather not know. People talk about how they can learn from everything, even when things are awful, they can come through it happy; but there are some things that could happen to you that you would give back to Fate if you were given the tiniest shadow of a chance."

A phantom flitted around the edges of my consciousness, like that proverbial "little bird" telling me he was probably right, that I didn't understand the darkness some people could quarter deep in their souls without giving an outer hint. Still, I hadn't liked her when I'd met her; I could tell something was wrong with her. I figured maybe she had been cold to him, maybe she'd didn't trust him when he told her what the Bauers were doing to him, maybe she'd even slapped him once or twice. His tone told me it was something else, something that perhaps I didn't want to know, a knowledge I would wish I could send back.

I inhaled slowly and listened. I heard something that chased the "little bird" away. It was that still, small voice: Our Father telling me to ask anyway. Maybe I didn't want to know, but J.D. needed me to hear it. "J.D.," I said, realizing I was crying, "you're my friend. I love you, and that is a very big deal to me. I want to listen to everything you need to tell me."

I brushed away my tears and looked at him. His eyes were closed, and he was biting down – hard – on the inside of his cheek. All was silent for a moment, then I asked quietly, "Do you want to talk about it?"

He nodded, the slightest bob of his head. "It's…it's not a comfortable thing to talk about," he told me. He was trying to figure out how to say it. I nodded and waited silently. "She wanted me…She asked me to…"

In a rush, I understood what he couldn't say. I got it, and why he couldn't get it out of his mouth. I felt sick. I had to resist the urge to gag. "I get it." I told him, hurriedly. "You don't have to say…"

He opened his eyes to look at me and saw from my expression that I did understand. He nodded and sighed.

"Did you tell anyone?" I asked.

"Her director. He talked to her, and she told him that I'd misunderstood. I knew I hadn't because of what I'd been told by other kids - boys whose cases she had. Besides, I'm not stupid, even if I sound it. I mean, I know how I sound, but…anyway, she told him it was a role-playing exercise, because of what happened when I was little. Did you know about that?"

I hadn't exactly, but I had guessed and tried not to think about it. "My Dad said the guy you lived with was killed in prison because of what happened to you."

He nodded. "As much I really disliked the guy, I don't feel good about what happened to him. I'm not vindictive like that. But his cellmate had a son in foster care; when it came out why he was in prison, this cellmate…I think in a way he felt he was protecting his own kid."

"That makes a strange kind of sense," I agreed softly.

"But it was bad stuff, and Keenan told her director she wanted to keep it from happening again, like so I'd know how to protect myself or whatever. But I knew she'd done the same thing to other kids. They wouldn't always tell her no, but I said no and got sent to the Bauers. She knew about him before. She knew he beat up on kids and let them go hungry, and she knew he kept them working until they passed out. She knew; he was the biggest reason she usually ended up getting what she wanted. But I couldn't change my mind. Four years in that place, and I couldn't change my mind."

My heart felt like it had been stepped on or left on a train track. I was crying again, and I wanted to give J.D. a hug so badly that my arms shook from the effort of stopping myself.

"It's kind of ironic, because she got away with that because of what happened before. But that was the same reason she didn't get what she wanted from me. I couldn't give in because of those four-and-a-half-years with Mr. Better Run, Mr. Tuckduckandroll himself. What happened then…never my choice. I didn't have any control; I didn't understand what was happening. Once I grew up, once I got strong enough, I promised myself it wouldn't happen again like that, not until it was my choice, no pressure."

I had been watching his face while he spoke, and most of the time he wasn't looking at me. He would look at his hands, his feet, the ceiling, the bed, the floor, but rarely at me. Then he stopped talking, and his eyes met mine. His gaze became so intense, I felt he was looking through me. I wondered if he was seeing me at all or if he had let his eyes go out of focus. I was the one who looked away; I couldn't take it, so I glanced away for half a second. When I looked back, his eyes were peering around the ceiling, as if he was searching for his thoughts there. He must've found them, because he picked up where he left off.

"I knew it wasn't right, and I decided it wouldn't happen until it was right. I still don't know what that means; but I promised myself I would before I let it happen again."

78

"You didn't let it happen," I told him.

He nodded. "It wasn't my fault then. I know. A lot of kids who are abused that way blame themselves. I don't. But I know if I have that type of relationship in the future, I will be responsible for it being right or wrong. So I promised." He sighed and shrugged again. "Not that it matters. I mean, I can't even…" His voice faded, and I thought of all the things he might've said then: "I can't even shake someone's hand" or "let my friend give me a hug". He sat tracing designs on the blanket with his finger and looking miserable, and my heart broke for him.

"I'm sorry to make you go through this," I told him.

"It's okay. If you want to hear it, I want to tell you. I don't wanna feel like I'm hiding from you, or from Mark and everybody. You are my friends."

"Sure. And, anytime you need us, we're here. Well, at least, we'll drop everything to get to where you are."

He nodded quickly, and I could almost see tears forming in his eyes. That was different, because a lot of the time, J.D. seemed detached from his emotions, like he only felt them as much as a random person sitting next to him would. More like he was a witness to his abuse than the victim himself. Feeling things deeply enough to cry about them was not normal for him at all. I realized feeling like that with me there would make it harder for him, so I stood. "I should get back," I told him.

I turned to leave but stopped, reaching for the Bible on his nightstand and handing it to him. "If you still want your answer," I said, "about…well, you know…it's in that Book. Who knows? Maybe you'll find whatever else it is you're looking for. I hope you do." He took the Bible, looked at it, and shrugged.

Before I left, I added, "J.D., Keenan's not in control. God is."

Chapter nine −

When I got home, my dad and his older sister Ceara (Ingrid's Mama) met me at the door. "You slapped Ingrid?" my father asked me. He'd always checked Ingrid's stories of abuse with her alleged abuser before doling out punishment, because her claims were often unfounded.

"Yeah," I answered directly, without even a blush or the tiniest duck of my head. I'm ashamed to say I was almost proud of it at the time.

"Why did you do that?" my father asked. He was still dealing calmly and rationally with the situation, but Aunt Ceara was getting close to blowing the proverbial gasket.

"She can't treat other people with respect, and she doesn't deserve to be treated with respect herself," I explained.

Ingrid had walked up while I was explaining myself, and she scoffed at my statement. "It's me who can't treat people with respect?" she said. "What about Mr. Antisocial Glutton Freak?"

"I'll slap her again," I said.

"Ingrid, please be quiet for a minute," he said. The sulky look returned to Ingrid's face, but she shut her mouth. Dad looked at me and asked, "What is this about?"

"J.D.," I told him. "He came over today, remember? He asked yesterday, and I told him if he wanted to come, he was welcome. We had gifts for him, anyway. So he came, and from the second he walked in the door, she was all over him. You know how he is about that kind of thing. He kept edging away from her, and it ticked her off.

"Then he leaves, and Ingrid and I go to my room, and she starts attacking him. She was calling him rude, arrogant. A glutton, she said. Revolting. She told me he was like plastic food - all look, no substance. You know J.D., Dad. He has more substance in his fingernails than she has in her entire being."

I took a deep breath before going on, "I'm sick of her. It's been an entire lifetime of criticism and shallow arrogance with Ingrid. For years she's been calling Mark a geek and a nerd and telling me that I need to get cooler friends. Now she meets J.D. and accuses me of being superficial. And she was picking on J.D., Dad. Little Boy Lost who's spent his life-" My voice choked off abruptly at that point, but my thoughts continued to the end of the sentence: who's spent his life suffering every type of abuse and harassment at the hands of the people who should've protected him. I sighed, suddenly feeling the draining effect of not only the fight with Ingrid but also of the things J.D. had told me while I sat on the floor of his bedroom.

"By the way," I mentioned, offhandedly. "He asked me to tell you thanks for the watch."

Dad nodded and thought for a second. "I think it would be best," he said finally, "if the two of you didn't discuss J.D. But Ingrid, I would like to say Jay Dillon deserves a lot more credit than you've given him. His actions today had nothing to do with arrogance. For reasons I wouldn't feel at ease discussing with you, he isn't comfortable with physical contact. His strange eating habits probably have to do with the fact that he's been starved before. But he's a decent kid. I respect him. I will not listen to you tear him down, and neither will my wife nor any of my children. I think the same would go for my brother and his family, as well. Do you understand?"

Ingrid (having the grace to appear ashamed, though she probably wasn't) looked at her feet and murmured a vague affirmative. My father wasn't going pick at her lack of enthusiasm. He gave a curt nod and said, "Good." Ceara and Ingrid left, and Dad looked at me and said quietly, "Never attack unless you are in danger. Enjoy your Christmas, but we are not done."

*****

The next day, I woke up early from a bad night's sleep and headed over to Mark's house next door. Mark and I headed down to the basement under the guise of checking out a new computer program he'd gotten for Christmas. Huddled on an old couch, I choked out what I had learned the day before. He listened, without comment, until I was finished. "That's really sick," Mark said. "How old was he?"

"Barely thirteen. Younger than Tierney."

"Ugh." He was shocked. "What kind of person...? Thirteen-year-old kids...What kind of person...?"

"The evil kind. So what can I do?"

"What do you mean?"

"Well, she belongs in jail for what she did to him and to the other boys. And what if she does it again?"

"Well, you can pray she doesn't. Or that she'll get nailed if she tries."

"Yeah, but..."

"Anna, you have evidence?"

"Don't you believe J.D.?"

"Yeah, but I can't do anything about it. FIA didn't believe him, and the judicial system won't believe us simply because he told us."

I gave him a miserable look.

One of his strong brown hands patted my trembling pale ones gently. "Annie, you're used to being everyone's big sister.

You like to protect people, so I know this is extremely frustrating for you."

"Yeah, imagine how J.D. feels."

Chapter ten –

At lunch on the Monday after Christmas break, my friends and I were sitting at our usual table in the cafeteria when Vanessa floated over. She hovered with a clipboard in her arms at the end of the table where I was sitting across from J.D. "Hey, Aenee!" she greeted as she set a copy of my talk in front of me, letting it get dangerously close to a squishy landing in my chocolate pudding cup. J.D. raised his eyebrows at Vanessa's botched pronunciation of my name. I shrugged and wrinkled my nose. "Your talk is, like, approved and everything!" she went on. "The Retreat Board was pleasantly surprised. They thought you'd write something too preachy."

I almost cringed at her statement. "Great," I responded without a hint of enthusiasm.

Vanessa gave me a cheese ball smile and turned to J.D. She was suddenly putting on *that* type of air, like he was the only element in the universe to her. I could tell the attention was making my friend feel nervous, though he hid his nervousness well. "Mr.

Foster," she said, her squeaky voice suddenly becoming smoother. "I don't believe I've heard what your first name is."

"Jay," he answered, simply and flatly.

"Just 'Jay?'" she asked in a candy-coated tone.

"Everyone calls me J.D."

"J.D.? I like that."

He gave a tight smile and shrugged. Some guy across the cafeteria shouted Vanessa's name and waved her over. She gave a goodbye, a saccharine smile, and a Miss America-type wave, all three of which were directed at J.D. Then she twirled in the air and floated away. My friends and I breathed a collective sigh of relief. "I think she likes you," Juli informed J.D.

He groaned.

"I'm glad you feel that way," Ben said, "because you're my friend, but I'm not going to start hanging out with Vanessa Montgomery."

"Yeah," Juli agreed. "She has all the glowing personality of..."

Ben finished for her, "...Peanut butter."

"Hey!" J.D. said in a defensive tone.

"What?" Ben asked.

"You like Vanessa?" Juliana quizzed.

"No. I like peanut butter."

"Yeah? Do you want my peanut butter crackers? I'm full."

"No, thanks. I'm full, too."

I could've applauded him for that.

*****

As J.D. and I were heading to our French class, he asked me, "So what's that 'talk' thing?"

"Oh, that." I explained about the Junior Retreat and the motivational speaking program and told him I was giving one of the talks.

"Motivational speaking?" he asked.

"Yeah," I confirmed, not sounding motivated at all.

"Well, you're good at that, Annie. And I should know."

"Yeah, well…" I sighed.

"You're not excited about the 'talk?'" he questioned.

"Not really," I admitted.

"Why?"

"My talk is a cop-out."

"What do you mean by that?"

"Well, this may sound kind of stupid, but I want to make a positive impact on Lincoln. It's my 'divine calling,' if you will, for this time of my life."

"That's not stupid," J.D. told me. "More people should be trying to do that. But I don't see the connection. What does that have to do with your 'cop-out' talk?"

"The talk is about fears and dreams. I know the only thing that can banish fears and offer real hope is God, but my talk doesn't say a thing about that. It says the exact things the motivational speaking committee and the Junior Retreat oversight board want me to say. A load of nonsense about how writing your fears out on paper helps you focus on conquering them..."

"Blah, blah, blah," J.D. supplied.

I nodded. "It's utterly worthless."

J.D. gave me a thoughtful look before saying, "Well, maybe you should just scrap the talk on that paper and, to exploit a grossly over-used expression, 'speak from your heart.'"

"The thing is, that could get me in deep, boiling water with the talk board and the retreat oversight committee."

He shrugged. Sometimes that apathetic gesture of his intended to convey a lot more meaning than you would think. It could punctuate his words rather than underplay them. He said, "Well, of course you have to answer to boards and committees, but who else do you have answer to?"

Chapter eleven -

Sarah and Kieran brought Shelby to visit her grandma and grandpa in early February. I went over to visit J.D. and play with the baby. I love babies, especially ones that aren't related to me. They're cute and funny; and when you get tired, you give them back to their parents. It's a great system. Sarah, once again, asked J.D. if he wanted to hold Shelby, and he declined. I asked Sarah if I could pick Shelby up. "Of course," she told me.

I smiled and lifted the baby in my arms. "Isn't she precious?" I asked J.D., tilting her so he could see her face. "Look at her tiny feet and button nose."

He laughed softly. "She's got my sister's smashed-up nose." He teased loud enough for Sarah to hear, before lowering his voice. "She is sweet, though."

"Yeah, and too little to realize that either of us exist really."

He gave me a quizzical, yeah-so-what's-your-point look.

"She can't hurt you, J.D.," I explained. His blue eyes widened and looked from my face to the baby's. Shelby's eyes cracked open for just a moment before closing again. She sighed.

"Do you want to hold her?" I asked J.D.

He bit his bottom lip and gave a jerky nod. I smiled but was able to contain most of my joy at the fact that he'd finally agreed to touch another human being. I gently transferred the baby to J.D.'s arms, being careful not to bump him in the process. He accepted her awkwardly, but soon shifted her safely and snugly into one arm. He brushed his free hand gently over her silky, blonde hair, lifted her hand, stared at her fingers for a moment, and tickled the bottom of her foot. A couple minutes later, he suddenly shoved her towards me. I hurried to take her because he looked about ready to dump her, either into my arms or onto the floor. "Is something wrong?" I asked, still trying to get a good hold on the baby.

"She's getting hot," he muttered.

"Like a fever?" I asked, confused. She didn't feel feverish to me, and she certainly wasn't acting like my baby sister had when she was sick.

"No. It's...nothing. Never mind. I just didn't feel like holding her anymore."

It was a lame cover-up. I looked at Shelby and happened to glance over at J.D.'s arms. They were flushed bright pink, like a bad sunburn. I hid my thoughts, but I was quite confused.

When I got home and told Dad about it, he said it was probably some kind of psychological reaction. Dad said J.D. probably knew most contact with other people didn't cause actual physical pain, but the abuse had taught him to be afraid. Likely that somehow seemed more tangible than knowing in his mind the pain wasn't real - thus the flinches and redness. I thought and prayed about it, because I wanted it to stop. That might've been partly selfish, because I wanted to be able to give him a hug whenever he said something that broke my heart. With all the words in the world, sometimes I can't think of better comfort than a gentle touch.

*****

"Doesn't Vanessa have a boyfriend?" J.D. asked me after school the next day. We were at my locker, and I was kneeling by my backpack, packing up to go home. I stood and thought for a second. Who was dating whom at Lincoln was a difficult question, because many kids changed boyfriends and girlfriends about as often as they changed socks. But if I remembered correctly, the relationship between Vanessa Montgomery and her "trophy boy" had remained pretty constant for about eighteen months.

"Yeah," I told J.D. "Adam White."

"I don't know him," J.D. told me.

"He's a quarterback for Lincoln's varsity football team. He's in our French class. Big guy, dark hair and eyes. The kid who's somehow making a B, even though he still hasn't learned simple phrases like *Sil vous plait* and *C'est la vie*."

"Ah, him."

"Why do you ask?"

"Well, I thought she was with somebody, and it makes me wonder why she won't leave me alone. That's what I really want to know."

"Gee, I can't guess."

"Okay, I'm detecting a note of sarcasm in your voice, Annie, but I'm going to ignore it so we can talk about my problem."

"I'm sorry J.D. I don't know what I was thinking."

"Now you're being patronizing."

"Talk to me; okay? Your problem…" I prompted.

"She's found out where my locker is, and she waits for me after every class. I want her to go away, and I've tried everything. I give one-word answers to her questions; she says I'm shy, and that's cute. I ignore her, she says I'm playing hard to get, and that's cute. I finally tell her to leave me alone, she laughs, that's cute. She has a boyfriend. Why does she bother me?"

"She's said that clearly; she thinks you're cute."

"Why?"

I shrugged, shoving a book into my bag. "Don't ask me why Vanessa Montgomery thinks anything that she thinks. She and I receive data on different wavelengths. We don't agree on anything." Except, I thought to myself, he is cute.

"Why won't she take at least one of the rather obvious hints that I've given and go away?"

I could answer that question. That was one thing I understood about Vanessa that she probably didn't realize about herself. "Ah," I said to him. "There's the thing. Walk with me, J.D." I zipped my bag and hauled it up onto my shoulder. I started hurrying towards the exit, and J.D. kept pace with me.

"So, you were saying, 'There's the thing…'" J.D. was prompting me now.

"Well, the thing with Vanessa is…" I paused and looked around to make sure no one was listening before I blazed forward. "…she has an egocentric view of our solar system. She thinks the sun, moon, and nine planets all run their orbits around her person."

"I know that. But what does that have to do with me?"

"A lot. Because, in Vanessa's mind, it isn't possible you wouldn't be interested in her, probably even more than she's interested in you. She probably thinks she's doing you a great act of kindness by favoring you with her attentions."

"That's crazy."

I shrugged. "A lot of people have a lot of crazy things going on their heads."

Case in point…

J.D. and I had to go to the store that evening to get construction paper, glue, and colored pencils for a project for French class. Jim was working late, Kieran had a business dinner, and Mrs. Jacobs and Sarah wanted to go to a ladies' tea, so J.D. and I offered to take Shelby along to the store. We picked up a few things for our parents and headed to the school supply aisles when Shelby woke and began to cry. J.D. picked her up and bounced her a few times before shoving her into my arms saying, "Here. You've done this before."

I accepted the baby, bounced her in my arms, and shushed her softly. I turned to J.D. and was about to tell him to go ahead and push the cart on to school supplies, when a lady came up to him and shoved a Bible into his hands. He got a surprised look on his face and held it out to give it back to her. "No, thanks," he told her. "I've already got one."

"Then give it to her," she said, nodding at me.

"She's got three or four."

"You two should read them."

"We do."

"Why are you still living in sin?"

J.D. gave her a look that said he had no idea what she was talking about, but it finally dawned on me what she was driving at. "This is his niece," I told her. "We're babysitting."

"Oh, well, the Bible says to avoid the appearance of evil."

"It also says you'll be judged in the way you judge others. My friend is trying to give yours back."

She wouldn't take it, so J.D. set it on a shelf, turned, and began to push our cart toward school supplies. I followed with the baby snuggled in my arms.

"What's wrong with that woman?" J.D. asked later as we loaded the car. "Why'd she assume Shelby was our baby?"

I shrugged. I didn't want to think about that. J.D. and I had just seen one of those "Christian" displays I never want a person who's searching for God to see. Judgmental legalism turns people off. "She made an incorrect assumption," was the only response I had to give.

"Yeah, well, 'incorrect assumptions' have been messing around with my life since I can remember. I'm sick of people assuming things about me. No one's ever given me a chance. I don't get it. Life is bad enough. Why would anyone want to assume the worst?"

"I don't know, J.D." I told him, honestly. "Not everyone's like that."

J.D. gave a weak smile and said, "I know. You aren't."

"Thanks," I told him. "You know what else? That type of judgment isn't a reflection of the One who wrote that Book. God knows everything; He doesn't make incorrect assumptions about people. And even when we do mess-up, even when we do it thousands and thousands of times, God has enough grace to cover it all – if we let Him."

J.D. gave me a comical pursed-lip smile and one of his trademark shrugs, closed the trunk lid, and headed to the driver's side door.

Chapter twelve –

J.D. and I worked on the French project that Saturday. We were almost done by 4:00 p.m. when Ben called. "Juliana's upset about something," he explained. "She got mad and yelled at me, and she won't tell me what's wrong. Will you talk to her?"

"Yeah. When?"

"Is now okay?"

"Sure."

J.D. and I agreed we could finish the project the next day after church, and he offered to take me to Juliana's since Mom had taken my car in for a tune-up. Juli wasn't home, and her mom told us she'd gone for a walk, so we got back into the car. About four-and-a-half blocks away, we saw a Miata full of teenage boys parked at a corner. Kevin Sheridan, one of Lincoln's varsity football kickers, had gotten out of the car and started shouting things I won't repeat. We looked and saw Juliana sitting on the curb and looking as if she wanted to disappear. J.D. parked the Saturn across the street from the Miata, got out, and ran to Juliana. I followed close behind. "Hey," J.D. called to Kevin. "Are you blind or just stupid? Where do you think you are? Move on."

Kevin got all puffed-up. "Excuse me?" he asked, as he stood up straight, taking a step toward J.D.

I noticed an almost imperceptible change in J.D.'s posture, which clued me in to the fact that he was prepared to defend himself. "Leave," J.D. answered, calmly and firmly. Kevin tried to throw a punch, but J.D. caught Kevin's arm and moved, twisting Kevin around so he was facing the car with his arm pulled, painfully, behind his back. Kevin was shrieking long before J.D. used his other hand to grab Kevin's neck and pin his face to the hood of the Miata. After that, J.D. mercifully let go, but his expression held a warning. Kevin stood for a moment, watching J.D. and rubbing his arm. J.D. opened the Miata's door, turned, "helped" Kevin into the car, and slammed the door behind him.

"Go," J.D. ordered through the open window. Kevin immediately put the car in gear and drove off. Once they were gone, J.D. went back and sat down on the hood of his own car.

I sat down on the curb beside Juliana and put my arm around her shoulders. "Ben called me," I told her. "He's worried."

She didn't say anything.

"Ben and I only want to help, you know."

"I know. But you can't really."

"We can pray."

"You can pray without knowing."

"Whatever it is, Juli, I'm sorry."

"It's not you."

"I know; if it was, you'd tell me. But I'm still sorry."

"For what?"

"That life can hurt this bad."

"You're too caring, Aine."

"That isn't possible." I squeezed her shoulder and asked, "Want me to walk you home?"

"No, I need more time. Could you tell Ben that I'm sorry?"

"Sure."

"And tell J.D. thanks for getting rid of Kevin."

I nodded.

"Thanks, Annie."

"You're welcome, Juli. You always are."

She gave me a weak smile. "I'll be fine."

I knew she was telling the truth. I know she's tough, even though everything one can see about her says she's like a flower. She's a small, delicate-looking person who's surrounded by all sorts of color. She looks like she'll be blown away in the next storm, but I've been through storms with her, and she is the only flower ever made with steel reinforcements. Still, it was hard to let go of her shoulder and walk away. I felt so weak and frustrated. I couldn't help her anymore than I could help J.D.'s "sunburns." The big sister in me didn't like that at all.

Chapter thirteen –

"Guess what happened," Mark said as he appeared at my locker Monday before school.

"Your parents finally bought you the baby elephant you asked for when you were three?" I guessed. I loved this game. Today, I decided on an animal theme.

"No." Mark would regret saying "guess what" to me before this was over.

"Your cat had kittens?"

"I don't have a cat."

"Your dog had kittens?"

He gave me an incredulous look.

"Your dog had puppies, then?"

"Duke is a male, Annie."

"Your canary laid eggs?"

"Please, Aine, just give up."

"I give up," I announced, as if it was entirely my idea.

"Thank you. Anyway, I was at State Street Joe's yesterday," he explained. State Street Joe's is a local, internet coffee house.

"They were having problems with their WiFi, and Jack Lewis, the owner, paid me to come fix it. I was almost done when Adam White came in, bought an espresso, and sat beside me."

I stared at him. "Why?"

"I'm getting to that. First, he asked about Vanessa's interest in my friend Jay. It took me thirty seconds and a few questions to figure out he meant Vanessa was hanging around J.D. I finished up my job, told Adam I was sure J.D. wasn't interested in Vanessa and that I hadn't noticed her interest in him, except once in the cafeteria."

"Adam's right, though. She's really been bothering him, hanging out at his locker and stuff like that."

"Really? J.D. hasn't told me that."

"Yeah, well. Anyway, you were saying about Adam…"

"Yeah, so I tell him I don't know, and I wait for him to leave. I had some homework, so I was pretty anxious to get home, but he didn't go."

"Why not?"

"I'm getting to that. After we had that discussion, he kind of just sat in his chair, and I figured he wanted to talk about something else but couldn't think of how to bring it up. I almost just got up and left, but Something told me to wait."

"Did he finally talk? What did he want to ask about?"

"God."

I coughed, a maneuver I'd learned to prevent my jaw from dropping open. "You're kidding."

"No, he asked about Jesus and all that. We sat and talked for over an hour while he asked me all these questions about what I believe."

"Wow."

"I know. I almost went into shock where I sat. But pray for Adam, because, from the way he was talking, it sounded like he was close to getting it."

I nodded. "I will definitely do that."

"By the way, I told him he could ask you questions too, if he wanted." He grabbed his bag and disappeared before I could respond. I was surprised, but at least Mark had given me some warning. Really, Adam or anyone else could've come up to me at any time, without any warning at all, like he'd done to Mark yesterday. Usually I wouldn't get even the measly twenty minutes of warning I got this time.

In choir, we had a study hall. Mark and I were sitting together, talking quietly. We were mostly honor students in choir, and I don't know why, it being first hour on Monday, we were expected to have homework to do. I had just finished telling Mark about my weekend when Adam White came up to talk to both of us. "So," he said, "Run through this whole Jesus thing with me one more time." Just like that. It was strange. He said it almost like he was asking if we knew last season's top ten A.L. batting averages. "The whole thing," he continued. "From the beginning."

Mark and I stared at him for a moment. We were kind of surprised at both the content and delivery of his question. I actually started talking first. The words just flowed out of my mouth, my tone holding that same strange matter-of-fact tone with which Adam had asked his question. "Well," I began, "that story started a long time before Jesus was born. You know, God created the world; Adam and Eve, the first people, had a perfect relationship with God 'til they disobeyed him. That's sin, and sin separates people from God, kind of like a divorce. Now God has three parts or 'persons': the Father, the Spirit, and the Son, that's Jesus. And Jesus is God's way of winning out over sin and giving people a way to get back to Him."

I stopped, and Mark continued, "See, God promised people a way back to that perfect relationship with Him thousands of years before Jesus was born. He said a person, called the Messiah, would make possible reconciliation between God and people. As the years went by, He gave more and more clues so the people would recognize the Messiah when he came. Among other things, it was said that his mother would be a virgin when He was born-"

"A virgin?" Adam interrupted.

"Yeah."

"But who was the father?"

"God," I told him.

"So Jesus was a demigod?"

"No, He is one hundred percent God, one hundred percent man, fully both. We don't understand exactly how that works, but…"

Adam shrugged.

"Anyway," Mark continued. "He was to be born to a virgin in the town of Bethlehem in Judea. His death was also prophesied; and Isaiah says that his whip-lashings would be our healing. While He was being crucified, a process where the soldiers usually broke the victim's legs so they would die, not a single one of His bones would be broken. Most important, the Messiah would be resurrected on the third day."

"Resurrected?"

"Risen from the dead," Mark said. "Remember the whole empty tomb discussion we went through yesterday?"

"Oh, right. Just a little confused by the jargon."

"Understandable," I told him.

"So, then Jesus came…" Adam prompted.

"Yes. Jesus came," Mark said. "He was conceived immaculately, born in a barn in Bethlehem of Judea. He was crucified, but He was already dead when the soldier came. Because of this, the soldier speared Jesus' side and left his legs unbroken. After three days, Jesus' tomb was suddenly empty. Jesus fulfilled these and many more requirements that God had set up for the Messiah in the first half of the Bible."

I said, "Hundreds of people saw him after his death. Then he left with a promise to return. Paul, who wrote some of the second half of the Bible, said the payment for sin is death, but God gives eternal life through Jesus. Because Jesus was innocent, his death paid for our sin. Because He lived after death, so can we. And because He lived in a complete and perfect relationship with God, we can do so, as well, when we follow his example."

"What do I have to do?" Adam asked.

"Believe it," I said.

Mark added, "All it takes is your faith in Jesus. That he died to save your life, so you could be free from your sins, not ruled by them anymore."

I explained, "When we turn our whole selves toward Jesus, we turn away from everything He doesn't want for us. That 'turning away' from our sins is what the Bible means when it says 'repenting.'"

"What else?" Adam asked.

"Everything else," Mark said, "is whatever you personally need to work out with God."

"So, I, like, pray?"

Mark and I nodded together.

"I know some of the stuff that's wrong in my life and everything, but I'm not sure about some stuff, and it might get complicated."

"That," I began, as I pulled a Bible out of my pack and handed it to him, "is why there's a handbook."

*****

It's funny how people will check something out when someone they respect tells them it's okay to do so. Mark, Ben, and Juli had been my colleagues on the Lincoln High Project for a long time, ever since we arrived at Lincoln High, in fact. They each had "ins" in groups of kids at Lincoln where I wasn't involved. Mark had more access to the computer genius group; Ben was in on the second-string sports. Juliana was involved in some performing arts groups. But, with Adam, The Lincoln High Project had an in where it had never had one before – the popular kids. Adam commanded respect in that group, and he made that respect count. As soon as he "joined the project," some big changes started coming to Lincoln High.

Before Adam, openly admitting a relationship with Jesus was considered making a scene just as severe, or perhaps more so, than J.D.'s incident in social studies. Many of those who knew Jesus kept their mouths shut about it. When Adam White came along, it suddenly got a lot more socially acceptable.

Aside from that, watching Adam was cool. It had been a long time since I'd known a kid who was that excited about the whole Jesus thing, and it was contagious. He started coming to my youth group and bringing all kinds of friends. He got baptized. He read through the Bible in just over two weeks. He was always asking Mark and me questions about what he was reading. We had some great discussions about Bible stuff, and I was surprised I was learning a lot, too. A lot of other people at Lincoln were learning a lot, as well, because Adam was telling anyone who would listen what he was learning from the Book.

His attitude reminded me how vital Jesus was in my life. Like if you go for a long time without having deep, quality time with a good friend, you can forget how good it feels to stay up all night talking with them. And with God, it's bigger than that, because knowing Him was the reason we were created in the first place. Getting back to Him literally is having a date with Destiny. All around me, I saw this happening: old sparks like me getting stoked into bonfires and new sparks like Adam burning for the first time. I was amazed at the light.

As near as I could guess from later conversations, Adam was the twenty-fifth of that year's Lincoln juniors to make that date with Destiny, so to speak. Four weeks after Adam did, thirty-four kids who openly confessed Jesus were in Lincoln High's junior class. Before Adam, I'd known about ten. Several of Adam's friends from other classes had also become Christians. Mark and I had gotten to talk to some of them. It was cool seeing our efforts in Jesus name develop into God's miracles in His power. It was accomplishing something big. And I had no idea, but that was just the first spark.

Chapter fourteen ~

There were a few ways to get out of the Junior Retreat, and I had considered them all. The first way was getting barred for "behavioral violations," which I ruled out because my parents' response to such behavior was likely to be even worse than the retreat. The second way was to have failing grades in two or more classes, and because my parents have an accurate estimate of my intellectual ability, doing that was also likely to earn severe punishment. The third way was financial hardship, but Dad laughed when I asked him to quit his job. The final way to get out of the Junior Retreat was to have a previous obligation. I'd been begging my parents for two years to plan a previous obligation. It hadn't worked, and though a few dozen of my classmates had been excused, I was going.

The Junior Retreat is reportedly quite fun, and I had more friends in my class than I'd had before. Still, I would've rather spent spring break with my family. They weren't planning anything big, but they were going to spend a long weekend in Mackinaw, and I was sorry to be missing that.

Also, the traveling itself – to a resort in Orlando – would take more than twenty-four hours each way, and even though there were stops (like the one at a hotel where I would give my talk), it still meant a lot of time sitting either on a school bus or in one of three full-size vans. Then when rooming assignments were given, I found out that Juliana and I would be in the same condo as Vanessa and her lackey Denise. One good thing was that Mark, Ben, Juli, J.D., and I all got to ride on the bus together.

Before we headed out from the school, we heard the "Acceptance and Respect for Peers Talk," an expectedly disappointing speech delivered by one of the most popular and snobbish guys in Lincoln High's junior class. After that, my five friends, about five other kids, and I held a short prayer session while the rest of the class made their final preparations.

When we were done praying, we hurried to board our vehicles. My friends and I were the first kids on the bus, and we rushed to the back. Mark took the single seat in the far back of the bus. Ben and Juliana each took a bench seat in the row in front of him, and J.D. and I took the seats in front of them. Vanessa and Denise were the next to board. Vanessa glared at me and took the seat in front of J.D. Denise sat down in front of me.

Vanessa hadn't exactly loved me before, but she hated me now. Adam didn't think his relationship with Vanessa fit in well with his new lifestyle, since they didn't have their beliefs in common. He had broken up with her, and she blamed me. She was kind of grieving the loss of the long-lived relationship, but at the same time, she wasn't blowing opportunities to try to snag my blond and oblivious friend.

Lucky for J.D., he saw her coming. That wasn't surprising, though. He's blond, but he's not stupid. When she sat down in front of him, he crossed his arms over his chest, leaned his head back, and closed his eyes, wordlessly informing Vanessa that he intended to spend most of the ride in a coma, not flirting with her. Foiled again.

I smiled to myself and let my own eyes fall closed. J.D. hadn't yet, as he said, "invested his retirement in that Jesus thing," and sometimes I would get impatient. The fact remained, however, he hadn't completely dismissed the idea. He listened when we talked about God and hung around when we prayed. I knew he was reading his Bible, and he asked me questions sometimes. Even if he wasn't aware of it, he was searching for God, and I was optimistic. But God forgive me for how I smiled when he frustrated Vanessa.

Two hours into the trip, J.D. was motioning for me to move over as he scooted into my seat. He nodded at Vanessa, who was sulking behind the latest issue of People, and said quietly enough that neither she nor Denise could hear, "You aren't gonna ignore your roomie for the whole trip, are ya?"

The fact that Juli and I were rooming with Denise and Vanessa had become a source of amusement for Juliana's and my male friends.

"Shut up or die," I told him.

He laughed. I pretended I was preparing to sock him in the face, and he vaulted back into his own seat, snuggled down, crossed his arms over his chest, and pretended to go straight to sleep. It was going to be a long week.

"Dork," I fired over at the next seat.

Blondie grinned in his "sleep." A long week.

Chapter fifteen –

The retreat was on schedule, and there I was. My class had just eaten, and the build-your-own deli sandwich was not sitting well in my already nervous stomach. We were sitting or sprawling on the floor of the Northern Florida Hotel conference room, forming a sort of tired and lop-sided circle. Seventy-seven kids, nine adults, and one video camera all sat watching, waiting for me to speak. But I couldn't.

I forced a smile and looked around the room. Ben, Adam, Juliana, Mark, and J.D. had seated themselves close to me – my moral support. My notes were gathered in front of me in perfect order, but I couldn't speak, so I paged through them, as though I was still trying to organize them. I glanced at J.D., and he gave me a quizzical look that held more than a hint of challenge. I picked up my speech and stared at it, and I couldn't speak. I could hear J.D. asking, months before, "…but who else do you answer to?" I answered that question silently now. I answer to my own conscience and convictions, my Father…and His Son. Could I take His scarred hand in my own and tell Him, "I'm sorry I couldn't speak up for You; I was afraid of ostracism, detention, fill-in-the-blank?"

"If I know what You're asking, God," I prayed silently, "it's modern tantamount to that whole walking on water thing." I knew what He was asking. I sighed and let the notes flutter to the floor.

"That speech," I began, motioning to my notes on the floor, "contains exactly what every other kid in every other junior class at Lincoln High has been told at precisely this point, ever since the advent of the Junior Retreat. And I'm not giving it." I gave J.D. a you-won look, and he grinned at me. "Jay, over there," I continued, "is giving me a challenge, and I am taking him up on it.

"I'm telling you now, so you can leave if you like. I'm not trying to shove Jesus forcibly down your throats. People say different things now, but He never tried to force faith on anyone. He just told the Truth. Sometimes it made people angry, sometimes it still does, but that's all He ever did: tell the Truth. You are still free to believe whatever you like and go exactly where that takes you. I can't make you do anything; I can only tell you what I know.

"I'm not going to tell you lies. That's why I'm not giving that speech sitting on the floor. And I don't even need to tell you because you've already heard it repeated dozens of times. I'm going to tell you what I really believe about banishing fears and accomplishing dreams. Maybe you've heard it before; maybe it's brand new, but like I said, it's entirely up to you whether or not you take it to heart."

I looked around at Ben, Juli, Mark, Adam, and J.D. I wasn't up to looking farther than that; I wasn't ready to see what all the others had on their faces. My friends were all grinning, and I gave them a trembling smile in reply. I took a deep breath. "What a Truth it is," I murmured and added, not sure to whom I was speaking, "I hope you're ready."

My voice rose to normal when I said, "We need strength, power, hope, and lots of it to banish our fears and accomplish our dreams. Strength, power, and hope are three things we don't have on our own, things we can't manufacture in ourselves. We only have what has been given to us, as human beings, by our Creator. Every single person in this room as well as every person outside of it was born into weakness, fear, despair, and sin; and none of us have any power to change that. The only thing we can get for ourselves is death. We have no hope for anything but death if we're relying on ourselves.

"But God, our Creator, decided, in His own unlimited wisdom and love, to give us His strength, His power, His hope, and His life.

"Hope, I think, is the most important factor in what we're talking about right now. If you want to get rid of your fears and hold onto your dreams, all the strength in the world won't get you anywhere if you don't have hope. God offers hope, through the life, death, and new life of His Son Jesus, to any who will accept it and His Way for giving it. Jesus Christ died to pay for our sins and came back from the dead to give us the power to conquer them. In Him is our only real hope."

I stopped and looked around the room. A couple of the adults looked surprised and a few of the students looked annoyed, but most of the people seemed to be listening carefully. I kept talking. "If you want your fears burned in the bonfire tomorrow and your dreams buried in the garden to grow like all your siblings and friends have told you, go ahead, write them out, and give them to Vanessa Montgomery. If you want to pray for them and want others to pray for them, write them out, and give them to Juliana Huntington, Ben Wilson, Mark Ross, Adam White, or me. The five of us will also be available for the next..." I looked at my watch. "...twenty-five minutes if you'd like to pray with us. Thank you for your time."

As the students got to writing, I looked at J.D. "Are you happy?" I mouthed at him.

He nodded and mouthed back, "Aren't you?"

I grinned. I was. Terrified of severe disciplinary action, but happy.

When the kids began to finish writing, they started coming to pray with my friends and me, and I sent J.D. to the desk to ask for some Gideon Bibles. For almost half an hour, we prayed for fears and dreams and salvations. Dozens of fears and hopes were given to God in that time, as well as twenty lives. At seven o'clock, when the other kids headed off to other parts of the hotel to shop, swim, play arcade games, or whatever else they wanted to do, Adam, Ben, Juli, Mark, and I headed back to the bus to do some more praying. J.D. followed us out, and once we were seated in the bus, he shoved a stack of papers into my arms. "Vanessa gave me hers," he told me. "I thought you might want to pray for them too."

I nodded and glanced down at the stack, realizing it was only half as thick as the one my friends and I had collected. By a quarter 'til eight, we were all exhausted. We divided up the papers and packed them in our bags, and Adam went to his van to take a nap while we waited for the rest of the students. On the bus, the five of us curled up in our seats, fell asleep, and didn't even wake up when the rest of the kids boarded.

*****

J.D. and I walked into Grand Central Terminal, New York City. We bought our tickets, found our platform, and boarded our train with the other kids. We sat down, got comfortable and waited for the train to move. After a few minutes, it did move, and J.D. and I sat back to enjoy the ride. It was a normal class ride, really. Vanessa glared at me and gave *that* smile to J.D. Mark passed around his laptop. Ben and Juli did that too-cute tag-team talking

119

thing they do. Adam was explaining something from his Bible to another kid. Kevin was hitting on Denise and three other girls, at the same time. After a relatively short time, everyone got bored and settled into their seats.

We were in the first car, and, suddenly, a bright light lit up the tunnel. It was almost blinding, even towards the back of the car where my friends and I were sitting. We could tell the lights were from an oncoming train, but naturally we assumed the train was on a neighboring track. We soon found out it wasn't. The other train hit ours, and the front of the car was instantly several yards closer to me than it had been less than a second before. J.D. stood, grabbed his duffel, and said to me, "Aine, grab your bag. We gotta get out of here."

I woke hard from the nightmare, my green eyes snapping open to stare into J.D.'s anxious blue ones. "What?" I asked in confusion. "Did I scream out loud?"

"Get up, get your bag, get off the bus. We were in an accident. I smell gasoline."

I stared at him stupidly, and he grabbed my arm, pulling me up out of my seat. He handed me my bag, pointed to the bus's emergency exit, and gave me a gentle shove. "Go! Mark, Ben, and Juli are up the road a bit in the median."

Acting totally on instinct, because my brain wasn't working, I hopped out of the bus and ran toward my friends. J.D. followed with Denise and Vanessa. When I got to my friends, I dropped my bag on the grass and sat down on it. Denise drew close to us, saw my bag, gave J.D. an indignant look and said, "Why didn't you let us bring our bags? Look, even you have yours."

"Too much too carry," he answered, before adding. "We should get farther away." I stood, and we all obliged.

"But," Denise said, "all of you…"

"We have the papers," he interrupted. "From the talk tonight. Keep moving."

"Why do you need those?" Vanessa asked.

"I thought it might be nice, when they tally tonight's death count, to have something to remember the casualties by." Just as he finished, the bus exploded. Some shrapnel landed less than three yards from where we were standing. We stared at the flames. The three vans, all banged-up to varying degrees, were sitting in the median with bits of debris burning on the grass around them. People were standing around the vans and crying or walking towards us. I felt the tears begin to run silently from my eyes, and I fell to my knees.

Chapter sixteen ~

Only thirty-four out of seventy-eight students and four out of nine adults survived the initial impact between the tractor-trailer, the bus, and the three vans. Two students and one adult died en-route to the hospital. We were triaged at the hospital, and the doctors decided they couldn't do anything for one of the students. They gave him meds for the pain, and he died a couple hours later. Seven students were classified as critical. Five students and one adult had moderate injuries, and nine students and two adults had minor injuries.

As I sat in the ER waiting room, for some reason I couldn't help tracking this macabre numbers game of casualties and survivors. I guess at that time, seeing numbers was easier than seeing the lightless faces of my classmates. My mind wasn't ready to process the loss. It was hard enough to understand that my friends and I were hurt.

J.D., Ben, Vanessa, Adam, and I were on the moderate list. Denise, Mark, and Juliana were on the minor list. After two hours, all minor and moderate patients were still sitting in the waiting room while they dealt with the seven critical patients. Vanessa, who had a fractured forearm, whined for the hundredth time, "When are they going to help us? My arm hurts. That Tylenol didn't help at all. Why can't I get any care in this hospital?"

J.D. finally cracked. "Shut up!" he told her. "Don't you get that those doctors are trying to save lives right now? And you're complaining because your arm hurts? You can wait. The rest of us are sick of your screeching."

She was quiet after that, which made the rest of us happier. But less than twenty minutes later, we received the news that, while one of our critical patients was now listed in stable condition, another one of them had died. We cried all over again. Shortly after that, they came for Ben, to take care of his fractured rib and check out his abdominal pain. They set J.D.'s broken ankle and Vanessa's fractured arm. Another critical patient died, another was stabilized. They took care of Adam's broken hand and taped my broken fingers and put six stitches in my arm. It was on into the wee hours of the morning before they even got started on the minor injuries.

Parents started arriving about dawn. By that time, most the kids who had moderate or minor injuries had been released and carted by volunteers to a local church to get some sleep. Good intentions. But, sleep? Ha ha. J.D. was on some sort of prescription painkiller for his ankle, but I could tell it wasn't helping him a whole lot with his pain. He didn't complain, but I still felt badly for him.

Jim and Karen were among the first parents to get to Florida and to the church, and their presence lifted his spirits a bit. After Karen greeted J.D. and checked up on him, she told me she had contacted my parents in Mackinaw, and they hoped to be at the church by ten in the morning. That lifted my spirits.

The sanctuary of the church was quite a scene at that moment. It was full of crooning and crying and staring. What had happened was so unbelievable, yet so real. I started crying - again. Mrs. Jacobs put her arms around me and began to pray. I felt the faint pressure of fingers just barely brushing over mine, looked over, and saw J.D.'s "sunburned" hand withdrawing. I looked into those eyes and didn't see his pain anymore, only concern for me. I watched my friend for a moment longer before closing my eyes and joining Mrs. Jacobs' prayer.

*****

When I walked into the side door of my house on Sunday evening, my uncle Aidan met my parents and me at the door. Aidan is Dad's little brother. He's twenty-seven; and, since Dad's thirty-nine and my Aunt Ceara is forty-one, Aidan is actually closer to my age than theirs. Aidan's cool. From the time I was three until I was seven, he was my best friend (then I realized the kid next door, Mark, was a lot more convenient than a teenager who lived in Chicago). But he's still cool. A little weird, but very cool.

At twenty, Aidan dropped out of college, married a twenty-three-year-old second-year law student and got a job managing a mall toy store. Four years ago, Aid quit his job; and, while his wife Brigid bills, like, a million hours a week as a corporate lawyer, he stays home and (I quote) "plays with" his four adorable kids: Hannah, six; Micah, four-and-a-half; and Katie and Molly, one. Stated vocation aside, he does bring in a modest income inventing educational toys for a small toy company. "It pays the mortgage," he says. "Brigid pays for everything else."

Unlike my parents, grandparents, and Aunt Ceara, Aid never lived in Ireland. But having his sister, brother, parents, and my mom's family around all the time, Aid has a great Irish accent, as well as a natural American one. But unlike me, who only uses the Irish accent every once in a while to be cute or dramatic, Aidan uses it interchangeably with his American one. I don't mean that he switches his accent from conversation to conversation; I mean that he sometimes switches it from word to word. It's interesting, really. Now Aidan was hugging me and asking in that odd mosaic accent, "Hey, lass, how ya doing?"

I just stared at him.

"No, I didn't say that," he amended. "It would've been way too stupid. It was just your imagination."

"Great," I responded. "Now I'm hearing things."

He patted the back of my head, let me go, took a step back, and said, "I'm glad you came home." He smiled slightly, leaned in close, and whispered, "This is just between us, but you are my favorite teenaged niece."

I gave him a half smile, and he reached over to squeeze my shoulder.

"Why don't we go have a seat?" my mom said quietly.

The four of us moved to the dining room, and I collapsed into the nearest chair and felt my eyes leaking again. "Will Lincoln even need a whole class for us anymore?" I blurted. "There are only, like, sixty of us. Is that going to fill the three simultaneous junior classes and all the mixed-grade ones that we have running all day?"

"Well, I know it probably won't help a lot," Mom said. "But Ford High School's junior class is way over capacity. Next year Lincoln was going to get about half of Ford's extra kids from your grade, with the rest split between Taft and Washington. I'm guessing, but I think Lincoln will get all of the in-coming seniors now, almost seventy students."

"Sure'n they'll fit in good, too," I responded. "Vanessa Montgomery will make sure of that."

Mom, Dad, and Aid all just looked at me. "I was being facetious," I said.

Aid lifted his eyebrows. "Facetious?" he asked.

"I wasn't serious," I explained. "Vanessa's popular, and she'll make Lincoln High miserable for any kid from Ford."

"Oh," Aid said, nodding slightly. Aidan knows sometimes the best way to help people in crisis is to listen to all the mindless junk that comes out of their mouths. My mother reached over and patted my hand (the one that wasn't broken), and my dad told me it would be okay. I looked down at the stuffed, blue bunny sitting in my lap. The phone rang. "I'll get it," Aid said quietly as he stood to go to the kitchen.

Dad, Mom, and I were all silent, so we could hear Aid's side of the conversation from where we sat. "Hello?"

Pause.

"This is Aidan."

Pause.

"Well, that depends on who you wanna talk to."

Pause.

"No, you're right. I don't live here."

Another pause.

"Aidan O'Brien."

Yet another pause.

"Uncle."

And another. This one as Aidan came in with the phone.

"Really?" Aidan questioned the caller. "Ouch."

Short pause.

"Then you have developed a higher pain tolerance than I." Aidan reached over and handed me the phone. "It's your boyfriend," he told me.

"Boyfriend?"

"Said he'd drive over, but he can't on account of that broken ankle."

"Oh. J.D."

"Broken ankle?" Mom asked. J.D. had been boarding his flight home from Florida while my parents were de-boarding their flight to Florida, so they hadn't seen how he was doing.

"The doctors called it a clean break. Straight through, even with those army boots. He was walking on it right after the accident." I saw Aidan wince at that as I lifted the phone to my ear. "Hey," I greeted.

"Boyfriend?" I heard.

"Yeah, it means something different-" I kicked Aid in the shin "-in Ireland."

"Nah, I understand. You've met Daria?"

"She does that?"

"She's really interested in her little brother's non-existent love life."

"Yeah, well, Aid's not interested." I looked at him pointedly. "He's just insane; hears voices in his head."

Aid gave me a hurt, so-what-if-I-hear-voices-that-doesn't-make-me-insane look.

"He's right next to you, isn't he?" J.D. asked.

"Oh, yeah. So...what did you call about?"

"Just wondering how you were doing."

"Well, you know." I didn't have to explain; he understood. "How about you?"

"I'll survive. So will you. We have to."

I sighed. An awkward silence followed, and J.D. finally said, "So...I'll see ya."

"Yeah. See ya." I handed the phone to Aid, but was only vaguely aware he was having a conversation with J.D. The grief had gone away for a while when I was joking with my uncle, but I was feeling it again.

We got two other calls that night. One was from Florida, saying that another one of our critical patients had died, but the remaining two were stabilized. The other call was from Juli, asking if she could spend the night. "Don't you want to stay with your parents?" I asked her.

"No," she told me.

"Then it's no problem for you to come over, if you're sure."

"I'm sure. Could you maybe pick me up? I'd ask Ben, but his brother Hank came up from college, and Ben's missed him a lot since he left. Plus the rib, you know."

"Sure, I'll be right over."

Juliana was waiting in her front yard with her bag when I pulled up in front of her house. I asked her how her parents were handling the situation, and she shrugged. "I'd rather be hanging around yours right now," she told me.

"Not good?"

"My parents are normal, Aine. Yours, J.D.'s, Ben's are amazingly strong. The average Lincoln High parent is probably falling apart right now." I didn't respond, and we were silent until we got to my house and settled into the rec room with sleeping bags, blankets, tons of pillows, and my little sister (to cuddle with).

"What about you?" I finally asked Juli. "How are you doing?"

"Physically? Not too bad. Even better than yourself." She nodded at my right arm with the stitches and two broken fingers. "Just two stitches in my knee and a few scrapes and bruises. Emotionally? Not so great. All those people - mostly kids - are dead. Right after your talk, too."

"I know," I agreed. "They didn't get the chance to feel what it's like to grow closer to God, to understand Him better."

"No, they skipped right to the really good part." Aidan had come down to deliver some hot chocolate and cookies my mom had gotten ready for us.

"Hey, Aid," Juli greeted, before continuing, "You're right, but...it's just this hope thing. It's sad to...after..."

I continued for her, "After living an entire life without hope, die right after finding it."

"That's true. But it's sadder to just die without it. That Hope they had just found will help others, too."

"What do you mean?" Juli asked.

"Well, for instance, I would hate to wake up tomorrow and find out one of my children was dead. I love them all so much and any one of them, I would miss terribly. Hannah, my oldest, her sense of practicality, and the energetic desire for life that she has. Micah, my son, and his quiet thoughtfulness. The twins look who exactly alike but have incredibly different personalities. I'd hate to lose any of them, but it wouldn't end my life because of hope. If any of my kids died, I know I'd see 'em again.

"I have the same hope that's offered to the families and friends of the kids who died yesterday. I know what happened was a tragedy. It would be foolish to pretend it wasn't, but it would also be foolish to pretend God couldn't make a whole lot of good come out of it."

*****

The memorial service was held at Port Morgan's largest Catholic church on a Friday evening at the end of May, two-and-a-half months after the fact. The majority of Lincoln High's student body was at the service, as well as the school board, the staff, many parents, and many alumni, including the four Jacobs girls, who brought their families. They had pictures of all the people who had died on the wall behind the podium and in the program that was passed out. The platform was covered in flowers, and the large auditorium was filled to overflowing.

They read a poem that had been written by one of the survivors. They had people go up and discuss the lives and influences of the six teachers that had died. They had another couple of people talk about how the loss of fifty students had affected Lincoln High. They showed the video of the Junior Retreat, which was short. They had taken film of us while we were packing the bus, a shot of the pre-travel prayer session, boarding the bus, goofing off at the meal stops, shots from the rest period at the hotel where I'd given my talk, and that was about it.

Finally, Mr. Connor, the head of the Junior Retreat, stood up to speak. "Most years, the class on the Junior Retreat will hear well over a dozen motivational speeches or talks, as we call them, given by certain outstanding students in the class. This class only heard three. But, never, in all the years of the Junior Retreat, has a class been as inspired by the talks as this one. Never have I been as inspired by a talk as I was by the one I'd like to show you now."

Every eye was glued back to the screen that played the video. The screen blinked and lit-up, and I was up on the screen saying,

"That speech contains exactly what every other kid in every other junior class at Lincoln High has been told at precisely this point, ever since the advent of the Junior Retreat. And I'm not giving it." I was shocked, but the tape went on, all the way to my thanks for their time. Then the screen blinked again and closed its eye against a room filled with tears and stares.

Adam White stood up and gave a speech that was really a thinly-veiled revival sermon. That was followed by more tears. I had wondered why the service hadn't been scheduled in the school auditorium, but I realized none of that could've happened on school grounds.

After the service ended, my five friends and I were standing together talking when Kevin Sheridan came up to us, gave me a nasty look, and said, "Some trick you pulled, Ae-nee."

J.D. gave him an even nastier look and said, "Hey, you need some help finding the exit?"

Kevin turned toward the doors of the sanctuary, and J.D. followed him to make sure he got there. Ben then excused himself and Juliana to go home, and Adam left to find his parents. A couple minutes after they were gone, Vanessa appeared in front of Mark and me. "It's true, then?" she asked me. "Your talk, I mean." She looked around the room. "After all the playing I've done, I guess I'd learn to recognize real power when I saw it."

"Some people say God's a crutch for the weak," I told her. "Those people don't understand, because they don't have His bigger perspective. Needing God isn't the soul's equivalent needing a cane to get down the hall; it's like needing water to run a marathon. With Him, you can go farther than you've ever dreamed; but without Him, you waste away."

"Then I'm in trouble," she responded.

"Are you dead yet, Vanessa?" Mark asked, frankly.

She laughed, but it was humorless. "You know, sometimes, I think I actually am."

"If you're finally ready to come to life," I told her, "you are just in time."

So Vanessa Montgomery, the self-proclaimed first and last word on all things junior at Lincoln High found the real First and Last Word on all things everywhere. And even she was only the beginning.

Chapter seventeen ~

Every year since kindergarten, I'd looked forward to the last day of school, but junior year was something else entirely. I was never so glad to get out of that place. It had been a long year, and I was ready for a little break from disaster. The only question was would I get it?

When the morning of Monday the twelfth hit, I got a reason to doubt it. The "emergency" cell phone I share with Tierney (gotta love old-fashioned parents) rang at 6:00 a.m., waking me up. I wasn't going to answer it, but our voice mail was broken, and Tierney who sleeps like the dead was not going to hear it from his room. I picked up the phone and made a noise I hope vaguely resembled a hello. It was Mark. "Hello," he greeted.

"Oh. Hey, Mark," I told him with absolutely no enthusiasm whatsoever.

"Annie Eire. Guess what happened."

He sounded shocked and upset, so I started guessing bad things that could catch him off-guard. "Your computer has a programming problem you can't fix?"

"No."

"OPEC had another 'accident' and cut production again?"

"No."

"Lincoln decided to send our class on a repeat of the Junior Retreat this summer?"

"Please, just give up."

"I give up," I announced (as always, as if it were my own idea to do so).

"Hank Wilson, Ben's older brother, committed suicide."

I wasn't prepared for news that bad, and I sat in shock for a full minute before finally speaking again, and when I did speak, all I could say was, "What?"

"He killed himself."

He had to be joking. Hank had been depressed about something at college, but he hadn't done that. "Mark, that's not funny; that's sick. I'm surprised at you. I don't know why you-"

"I'm not joking, Annie. Ben's brother killed himself a couple hours ago."

"Then…why?"

"I don't know."

"But...how?"

"Shotgun in the face."

"Oh, man."

"Juli called and asked me to get everyone together. I'll call J.D. and pick you up in ten minutes."

We hung up, and I hurried to get ready. At Ben's house, he and Juli were sitting on the porch steps, even though it was raining. When Juli saw us, she patted Ben's knee, said something to him, and hurried to Mark's van to meet us. "Ben won't go in the house," she said. "The basement. It's bad, so we're sitting on the porch."

"Why don't we just sit in here?" Mark suggested. "We have breakfast. Annie's mom sent raspberry muffins, and Mrs. Jacobs sent coffee with milk and sugar."

"Sounds great," Juli said. "I've been up since four and haven't eaten a thing." She went to get Ben, and they climbed into the van. Ben looked like he was in shock, and it was strange seeing him that way. Of my friends, he'd always seemed the most solid; it was weird seeing him look so weak and small. We gave him a muffin and a cup of coffee, and he ate them, staring straight ahead and probably not realizing he was doing anything. When we asked him how he was doing, he said fine. But we all felt sort of like that. It was unreal. After everything else that had happened, this. And why? No idea.

*****

In the early afternoon, Ben went with his parents to a funeral home, and the rest of us went to Mark's house to wait. The Wilsons were staying with Mark's family, so they would come to the house after they handled some arrangements. Mark, Juli, J.D., and I went down to the sitting room in Mark's basement. We got settled, and nobody spoke until J.D. suddenly asked us, "Any of you ever thought about suicide?"

"No," Juliana answered.

"I get in moods," I told him, "but that has never really been part of it."

Mark said, "I came to the conclusion it wasn't a good idea. You?"

He nodded. "Sure. I wouldn't go the shotgun-in-the-face route; way too messy, blood and gray matter everywhere, and the funeral has to be closed casket because you don't have a face anymore, and-"

"Okay," Juli said, giving J.D. a pre-vomit warning.

"I think the easiest way would be to chase a little bit of heroin with a lot of alcohol. Basically puts you to sleep – you just never wake up."

Mark said, "Easy, assuming you knew how to get heroin."

"Oh, that wouldn't be a problem."

"You know how to get heroin?" Juli asked.

"Sure. Couldn't you guys get drugs if you wanted them?"

"If we wanted them," I said, "we could probably get marijuana."

"Yeah, we could get pot," Mark agreed. "We've been offered pot."

"But heroin?" I continued. "I'd have no idea."

"Did you ever try any of the pot you were offered?" J. D. asked.

"No," I said.

Juli shook her head. "Just the smell always made me sick."

Mark said, "I decided it wasn't a good idea. You?"

"Yeah, well, I'm not an addict or anything, but I've tried some stuff."

"When was the last time you've 'tried' something?"

"A year ago."

"Yeah?" I asked.

"That depends."

"On what?"

"On what you wanna hear and what you'd tell my foster parents."

"The truth, and nothing, because you're going to tell them."

"Six weeks ago."

"I guess I can give you that long to tell them, then."

He shrugged.

"Anyway," Juli spoke up. "Hank Wilson killed himself."

We were all getting uncomfortable with the conversation, and I personally felt stunned by J.D.'s admission. He and I had had a lot of conversations about extremely personal stuff, but that one had left me feeling like we could talk non-stop forever, and he would still have secrets. I was glad for a subject change and relieved when Mark continued the shift and said, "Yeah, we should pray for Ben and his parents."

We all stayed at the Ross house that night. The boys stayed in the basement, and Juli and I stayed in Mark's room. I wasn't sleeping well - a lot of tossing, turning, and troubled thoughts. I got up around midnight and went down to the kitchen to get a glass of water. On the way back, I had almost made it to the stairs near the dining room by the time I noticed J.D. was sitting at the dining room table. "Hey, Jay Dillon," I said quietly. "How long ya been there?"

He looked at his watch (I haven't seen him without it since we gave it to him for Christmas). "Forty-five minutes," he told me.

"Can't sleep?"

"Nope."

I pulled out a chair. Neither of us said anything for a while, then J.D. blurted, "Do you hate me now?"

I was surprised at his question. "No. Hating you has never even occurred to me. Why?"

"The drug thing."

"Oh, that. No, I don't hate you; quite the contrary."

"Huh?"

"It upsets me, but that's just because I'm worried. Drugs are dangerous. I don't want you doing something to screw yourself up."

"I'm already screwed-up."

"Nothing that can't be fixed."

"Yeah, well...I'll be careful, okay?"

I shrugged. "Okay. I guess that's fair. It is your life, and I'm the one that chose to get involved in it. Just think about the fact, if it'll make any difference just how careful you are, that a lot of people around here care about you. Me, Mark, Juliana, Ben. Your parents, your sisters, your nieces, my parents...Just think."

"I'll do that."

"I still think you should tell your parents."

He laughed, but not the amused kind. "Yeah, that'll go over great."

"Jay, they're not like the people before. They don't look at you like merchandise, like they can return you to the store at the slightest hint of malfunction."

"You don't understand how it works."

"Maybe I don't, but I know these people are different."

"Maybe it's not them. Maybe it's been me all along."

"You're not merchandise, J.D."

"I know that," he said, but his tone was flippant and insincere. He was patronizing me.

"J.D.," I said, and he looked at me. "You're not merchandise," I told him.

This strange look flickered through his eyes, then he closed them.

"J.D.-"

"Aine," he said. "Don't."

Something about his tone and the look his eyes had before he closed them convinced me I shouldn't push the issue. We were silent for another moment. I finally asked, "J.D., why do you think people commit suicide?"

He opened his eyes and gave me a thoughtful look. "I guess because they think life isn't worth the pain that comes with it."

"You think they're right?"

"Well," he said, "if they are, Someone's played a terrible trick on the human race."

I was a little surprised at that answer. "How do you figure?"

"Because, if one of us isn't worth it, then none of the rest of us are either, and... well..."

"We've all been fooled?"

"Exactly."

I thought about that for a second. "Interesting insight," I told him.

"Insight?" he asked. "I don't believe I've attained that level of intellectualism before."

I smiled and stood. "Then let's get to bed before you wax philosophical on us."

"Hey!" he said. "Don't insult the blond. It's not fair, 'cause he doesn't understand what you're saying."

I rolled my eyes at him. "Goodnight, J.D."

"Goodnight, Annie."

"Sleep tight. Don't let the bedbugs bite."

"Yeah," he said, laughing softly, "same to you."

And never, under any circumstances, I added silently, stick a shotgun in your face or shoot heroin into your blood. Always remember that we care, and, please, Jay, care back. Because that's another thing about suicide, it's probably the single most selfish, arrogant, and cowardly act a person can commit. It says, "Forget what I mean to anyone, or how it would hurt them to lose me; they're not important anyway. And, God, take your divine plan and just buzz off, because death is more worth my time than You are."

It's not right.

143

Chapter eighteen ~

Three weeks after Hank's suicide, Ben was taking counseling from his pastor and recovering as well as could be expected. With the grownups handling that situation, the rest of us had a chance to get a break from chaos. The strange thing was we'd gotten used to stuff going on and became bored silly.

Okay, may be not all the rest of us. Juliana was still dealing with stuff she wouldn't talk about. And J.D. was sleeping even more than he usually did and seeming depressed whenever he was around, though he made no complaints. I would've been happier if he had made complaints. I could've addressed complaints. I couldn't address silence, and J.D.'s silence was one of the things that helped drive me crazy for something to do, and I drove Mark crazy because I would've been lonely in crazy land by myself.

We needed something to do, so we started to try to think up ways to help J.D. But how do you cheer up a person who has been abused, feels unwanted, and doesn't even know who he is? We didn't abuse him, but we couldn't take away the past. We tried to let him know he was wanted, but that hadn't worked, so we decided to try to find out who he was.

Well, that decision itself was made kind of off-hand, but little events and changes in J.D.'s attitude led to it. In the middle of July, we got J.D. to come to my house for a movie night. Ben and Juli were both busy, so it was the three of us and my brothers and sister (Dad and Mom were on a date).

We popped in a movie, and Shannon colored. Mark, T.J., Boyne Andrew, and I played gin rummy, and J.D. curled up on the couch and stared blankly at the television screen. It took Shannon only minutes to get bored with her coloring. She dropped her crayons, went over to J.D., and did something that was sweet and manipulative at the same time.

Now I need to explain about Shannon. Shannon is not-quite eight and small for her age, has dimples, and a slight speech impediment (which J.D. relates to, of course). Those three factors make her seem even younger than she is. Plus, she has these curly, Irish red pigtails, bright green eyes, and freckles across the bridge of her button nose.

So she crawls over to the couch and props her chin on the armrest, about five inches from J.D.'s face. She gets this watery-eyed, half-smile, puppy-dog-pout, trying-to-look-happy-when-I'm-heart-broken look. J.D. tried to ignore her, of course, but she makes it difficult. He caved after fifteen seconds. "What?" he asked her (I'm a sucker for my baby sister, but even I don't give in that easily. J.D.'s a bit of a gullible moron when it comes to little kids).

"Dillon, will you play Monopoly with me?"

"I don't know, Shannon. I'm not sure I have the mental capacity for that right now."

"I'm seven," Shannon pointed out. "How much mental capacity do you need?"

"Probably at least enough to know my name," he countered.

Everyone in the room cringed. Shannon's bottom lip quivered. "Please," she pleaded.

"No, Shannon," he said, a bit sharper than necessary. She jumped, but it startled the rest of us, too. Then Shannon forgot and did the one thing she knew she shouldn't ever do. She reached out her little hand and touched his shoulder. It was J.D.'s turn to cringe. He jerked away from my sister and sat up. "Shannon…" he started, but he didn't have to finish, or even get a chance. Shannon immediately stood and fled the room.

Hearing my baby sister's hurried footsteps retreat up the stairs was what did it for me, and I appeared at Mark's door the next day to beg him to look for J.D.'s identity.

"I'm sure the police have already done that," he told me.

"The internet wasn't quite the same thing when we were three, Mark," I said.

"I know, but it's still an open case. It has been the whole time since."

"Yeah, but a cold one. As cold as they come, because nobody cared, Mark. And still nobody cares, except for us."

We set up at the computer in his basement. Well, Mark set up at the computer, and I hovered over his shoulder annoying him until he suggested I might want to go upstairs, fix myself a sandwich, and maybe watch a movie…or two. I went upstairs and tried to watch TV, and after an hour Mark came upstairs and told me to come down and see what he'd gotten.

"What did you find?" I asked once we were settled in front of his computer.

"Well, I searched missing kids, but I narrowed the search. Boys - well, duh. One who's now between seventeen and nineteen years old. Fitting J.D.'s description – blond hair, blue eyes, possible speech impediment. I found three – two missing along with one of their parents and one with a young woman not identified on the board, whom I assumed was the mother anyway. The first two had pictures posted. Neither was the little boy in the pictures J.D. got from his old social worker." Mark opened his browser and clicked on a link he had stored in his "Favorites" folder.

"I visited the third site. They hadn't posted a picture of the little boy. It focused on the young woman, but it seemed the person who'd created the site had no doubt they'd be found together. It isn't official. I figure they're probably not legally considered missing persons. It's on one of those 'Find Anyone!' search service bulletin boards. It's kind of weird the way it's set up. They do all of this stuff to protect everyone involved. They have an application process before they'll allow you to post your search. They find out who you are, who you're looking for, and why you want to find them. Then they'll only run information on the site they think is relevant to finding the person. They won't post pictures or names of children unless the searcher is the legal guardian of the child.   They don't list the name of the searcher, and they won't even list the name of the person being searched for if they know they're using aliases."

I watched as he scrolled down to the posting. I studied an old, grainy photo of the woman and read the listed dates while doing math in my head. The woman was a teenager in the photograph, but she had been almost thirty by the time the posting had been made. When Mark found the posting, it was five years old, and the woman had been missing nearly fifteen years. She had gone missing about a month before J.D. had been found in an alley in Lansing. I read snippets of the identifying information. *Using aliases Ashley Reilly or Riley Smith. Reddish blonde hair, blue eyes, five foot five, approximately 100 pounds. With a boy, age 3 at disappearance, 12 at date of posting. Email information to dreamsearch@aol.com.*

"I emailed 'dreamsearch,'" Mark told me. "I sent the picture of J.D. the police took right after he was found and asked if it was the boy they were looking for. I'll check now to see if I got a reply."
That minute it took Mark to log on and get his mail seemed to last

about six hundred years. And the only reply he got was from MAILERDAEMON, the address error reply service. The account dreamsearch@aol.com had been canceled.

"Why did they do that?" I asked Mark.

"Guess they found him."

"How? He lives half a mile from here and has no idea who he is."

"It's not him, Aine."

"Then who is he? We haven't found any other leads, Mark. It doesn't make sense. How does a three-year-old kid disappear in the United States of America without anyone noticing?" I felt myself getting choked up, but I promised myself I wouldn't cry.

Mark shook his head. "I don't know, Annie."

"What did we miss then? What did we not see? We must have overlooked something."

"Annie, it's over."

I choked on my tears.

Chapter nineteen –

After that, we did normal summer stuff. Mark was on vacation in August when Juliana came over to my house one evening. My brothers, Shannon, and I were bored out of our minds. My parents had us watching a documentary about Irish immigration and settlement during the nineteenth century (one of their "Get In Touch With Our Heritage" exercises, which they think is a normal summer activity for children as young as three).

I would have been asleep had it not been that the guy who was the authority on Irish settlement in Massachusetts was driving me absolutely crazy. For some reason I couldn't put my finger on, Mr. Massachusetts reminded me of Jay Dillon. Juliana popped in just as Mr. Massachusetts was starting in on another four-minute speech. "Can I hang out?" she asked.

"Sure," I told her.

"Do you want more company?"

"Why?" I asked, slowly and suspiciously.

"Cause I invited Ben and J.D. over for a movie night. I figured we gotta do something sort of fun while Mark's hanging out in Jamaica without us."

I shrugged.

She fell silent and watched the documentary for forty-five seconds before blurting, "That guy talks like J.D."

"That's it!" I exulted. "I have been trying to figure out for an hour why he reminded me of our blond friend."

"It's J.D.'s speech impediment - it makes J.D. sound like him. Just a little, though. Unlike his, J.D.'s voice doesn't, like, scream, 'Hey, I talk weird!'"

"But it's not talking weird with that guy," I objected, using my Irish Brogue. "It's just an accent."

"Whatever. But, anyway, J.D.'s voice does have a little of that 'awe' instead of short o thing, and he doesn't exactly over-emphasize his r's or l's either." Mr. Massachusetts finished his speech, and Juliana said, "But can't ya almost hear Blondie saying, 'Well, how'd'ya like them apples?'"

I smiled. "Sure'n I could."

"What apples?" Ben asked as he and J.D. entered the room.

J.D. said, "It's something you say to someone you don't like when you do something mean to them."

"It's a regional expression," Juliana said, nodding at Mr. Massachusetts on the screen. "And he's from the region." She wasn't planning on telling J.D. we were talking about his speech impediment; he is a bit self-conscious about it (Juli and I think it's cute).

Ben looked at the screen as J.D. went over and collapsed in the recliner (I gave him three-and-a-half seconds from fully awake to coma). "What's this?" Ben asked.

"*Irish Settlement in the United States During the Nineteenth Century*," I answered.

"Is this what we're watching?" he quizzed, skeptically.

"My mom wants us to finish it," Boyne Andrew told him.

"Just ten more minutes," I encouraged, tuning back into the documentary, feeling suddenly that I'd missed something important. "Could you rewind it a bit?" I asked Andy.

He gave me an incredulous look. "Why?" he asked.

"Mmm…Never mind." But I couldn't shake the feeling that some important information had hovered around the edges of my consciousness before floating away.

Chapter twenty –

Aidan brought the kids up to visit for a few days in August. Brigid was in New York City on a business trip, and Aid wanted a little adult company. Aidan has a certain presence – something about him tends to cheer me up. His babies don't hurt the vibe either, but I was really glad to see him. I was depressed - a vibe I was getting nailed with by J.D. It wasn't that I was seeing him looking all depressed. In fact, I hadn't seen him at all since the documentary party two-and-a-half weeks before. He'd missed church three weeks in a row because of a hide-and-seek stomach virus I think he can fake. I hadn't talked to him, as in a real conversation-with more than ten words-in over a month.

Besides everything going on with J.D., Hank Wilson was still dead. And that secret thing was still going on with Juliana. "Sometimes I wonder if having friends is worth all of the pain," I told Aid after I gave him the rundown. "Is that an evil, insensitive thing to say?"

"Well," he said, "I've felt that particular sentiment myself at times. But you feel it because it hurts, and it hurts because you care."

"Caring. That's the problem."

"Yeah, it's the problem. But it's also the answer." He looked at me and gave me a half smile that still made his dimples sink deep into his cheeks. The smile also made Aid look about as old as Boyne Andrew. I gave him a purse-lipped smile and sighed.

"You know what, though," he said as he reached to put his arm around me, and I leaned my head on his shoulder. "It'll work out. Maybe not quite the way you want. Maybe not when you want. But it will. Someday, you'll look back and see it went okay after all."

"I don't want to wait until someday," I told him. I was whining. "I wanna know now."

"I understand that, but what we want is not always right."

"How can it be wrong for J.D. to know who he is?"

"I'm not saying it's wrong. But maybe it's just not the right time. Maybe J.D. has to learn to accept himself as just J.D. before he finds out exactly where J.D. came from, you know."

I thought about that for a moment. "Maybe," I conceded. "But that may take a while."

"God has all the time in the world, so to speak. All the time in the universe, actually."

"J.D. doesn't."

"It shouldn't take that long."

"What can I do to help him out?"

"Well, I suppose the best thing is to just keep doing whatever you do that lets him know just J.D. is okay with you."

"It doesn't seem to help anymore."

"Just keep trying and praying. That's all you can do, Annie Eire, and that's all anyone expects you to do."

"It's not enough. Aidan, you met J.D. on Christmas and talked to him on the phone after the crash, but you haven't been around him for any period of time. It's so hard to express to him that I care about him. If I tell him, he gets uncomfortable; either he doesn't say anything or he changes the subject. I can't touch him, which rules out hugs, handshakes, and all that stuff. I can't do the spending-time-with-him thing when he's hiding from me. He used to come around all the time, now he doesn't want anything to do with me. It's almost like he's decided to declare war on my friendship."

"All you can do is keep trying. Maybe go around more. Hunt him down, perhaps." I snorted a laugh at the mental picture that last sentence gave me. Aid smiled at me. "Anyway, you can't force him to accept his life or God or anything else that he needs. You can't make J.D.'s decisions for him, Aine. You can only be his friend, and you have to accept that just as much as J.D. has to accept what he needs." He was right. I made a soft mournful noise. He tightened his arm around me briefly and gave me a kiss on the top of the head.

After Aid and I talked, I took his advice. First, I prayed. I asked God to help J.D. find out where he came from, to help me love J.D. and accept that was probably all I could do, and to help J.D. see that God loved him. Then I went to his house. Mrs. Jacobs let me in and gave me a hug. "Hello, Aine," she greeted. "How are you?"

"Good. And you?"

"I'm okay."

"Is J.D. here? I haven't seen him for awhile, and I was wondering how he was."

"Yes, he's here. I'm afraid he isn't doing so well. He's in his room, probably sleeping, but he should get up. I'll get him."

"Thanks. But...do you know what's wrong?"

She looked at me and tilted her head a little. "Well, at the core, it's the same old things. The sleeping all the time, the antisocial behavior, and the drugs are probably the same old symptoms, too."

"You know about the...um...drugs."

She gave me a rueful smile. "J.D. is the eighth teenager I've raised, Annie," she explained. "The pupils and the central nervous system don't react differently because of the 'y' chromosome. My husband and I are not stupid on any counts."

"He thinks you don't know."

"Well, J.D.'s used to parents who don't pay attention to him. We haven't mentioned what we know, because we're not sure what good it would do. I mean, how would we punish him? Ground him? He rarely leaves his room. Even if he weren't in his late teens and six feet tall, J.D.'s not the kind of kid one should spank. He's had enough of that. We know his drug use isn't habitual, at least at this point, and we think the thing J.D. needs most right now is unconditional love. We thought we'd hold onto the information until we could use it effectively." She turned to go to J.D.'s room, but turned back to me with a sort of mischievous smile. "If you would happen to mention that we knew, maybe…"

I nodded, and she disappeared around the corner into the hall.

J.D. didn't want to hang out. He didn't want to talk, he didn't want to laugh, and he didn't want me around. My friend gave senseless, one-word answers to all the questions I asked him. He seemed drowsy.

"Are you stoned?" I finally asked.

His eyes widened a bit, and I rejoiced silently that I'd gotten my first reaction of the day out of him. "No," he told me. We were in the living room, and he gave a meaningful look towards the doorway to the kitchen where Karen was making us sandwiches. "Keep it down, okay?" he reprimanded in a whisper.

I leaned forward and whispered back, "They know."

He leaned back from me. "What?" he asked.

"They know," I answered in a normal tone. "Karen and I were just talking about it before she woke you up."

"Aine, you said you wouldn't tell my foster parents."

"Actually, I've already given you more time than I said I would, but I didn't tell them."

"Then who did?"

"Believe it or not, they were smart enough to figure it out on their own."

"I don't believe it. If they know, why didn't they…ground me?"

"What would that accomplish? You rarely go anywhere, and if you did, grounding probably wouldn't stop you."

"You're right. Forget that. Who am I kidding? If they know, why am I still living here?"

"Because you're their son, J.D., and, contrary to your experience, people tend to keep their kids home, at least until they graduate high school."

"Don't try to feed me that, Aine."

I stared at him, wanting to yell at him and slap him and call him an idiot. He had a good thing in that house, and he still insisted on acting worthless. "You know what I don't believe?" I said, as I stood. "You. If you'd just open your eyes…" I held up my arms, palms open and turned to take in Jim and Karen's cheery living room and every other thing I could see from where I stood, including Karen in the kitchen making us lunch. "If you'd just open your eyes," I began again, "you'd see that…" But I couldn't finish. I sat, rather unceremoniously, down onto the coffee table and stared into J.D.'s bright blue eyes, for a while actually trying to hate him.

Neither of us spoke for a minute. Mrs. Jacobs delivered our food, and she didn't even ask me to move off the table. J.D. and I shoved down our food, grateful for an excuse to let the silence hang in the air like a bad smell.

When we were done eating, some sense of amiability returned. We talked for a while about things like the first day of school coming, our summer jobs, and the weather. But it was difficult for me to make small talk when we had so many serious things going on around us. I didn't stay long. When I made my excuse and got up to leave, I felt defeated, and he looked relieved. I thought again that it would be easier not to have friends than deal with that pain, but it was too late. My emotions were already hopelessly tangled-up with his. Caring was the problem.

Chapter twenty-one ~

When Lincoln High recommenced in the fall, my friends and I were back, bouncing around the beige cinderblock and green linoleum halls. We made it through half of the day all right, but were glad to collapse into our usual table in the cafeteria. As I started eating, I was thinking how great it was to have a usual table. With all the new kids from Ford wandering around the halls, I was glad I was still in the same place I'd been since ninth grade with the same people (plus J.D.) I'd been with since early elementary.

I was yanked from my musings when Mark fell in love. It was only ten minutes into the period, and everyone had been pretty quiet, each of us lost in our own thoughts, when Mark stood up. His book bag was knocked to the floor with a resounding thud. All my friends, except for J.D., who seemed engrossed in his peanut butter sandwich, looked up at Mark and stared as he, without a word of explanation, walked across the cafeteria to a girl with an obvious "alone-in-the-crowd" appearance. Mark said something to her; she watched him skeptically as she answered. They talked back and forth for a couple minutes before Mark pointed back toward our table where all of us but J.D. suddenly tried to look more like we were friendly and less like we were staring rudely. The girl watched us for a few seconds before shrugging and following Mark back to the table. "Hey, guys," he said as they reached us. "This is Amber Dennison."

We all gave slight smiles and light greetings, and Mark began to introduce around the table. "Amber, this is Ben Wilson, Juliana Huntington, Aine O'Brien, and Jay Dillon."

"Hi," she said lightly. "Nice to meet you...Well, I remember Jay from Ford, but..."

I nodded quickly. I was beginning to realize everyone from Ford remembered "Jay," but no one had really liked him. He had kind of been the school's official freak.

"Here," Mark said, pointing at the empty seat across the table from him, beside J.D. She started to the seat, and J.D. scooted away, probably seeming to her to be giving her more room. I knew he was giving himself more room, and I scooted away from him, also, so he'd be more comfortable.

We chatted awkwardly for a few minutes before a real conversation developed. We asked about how well Amber liked Lincoln and cross-referenced our schedules with hers. She was in one of Ben and Juli's classes in the morning, but they hadn't been introduced. She also had physics with Mark, J.D., and I right after lunch, business computers with Juli and Mark after that, and study hall with Mark last hour. Amber was glad to see she'd have some of her new friends around for the majority of her classes (I could relate; I had been relieved to find I had one or more of my friends with me for five of my seven class periods).

"Any classes with old friends from Ford?" Juli asked.

Amber bit her lip and shook her head gently. "My friends from Ford are still at Ford."

"I'm sorry," Juli said. "That must be difficult."

"A little," Amber admitted. "But I'm glad to meet you guys."

"We're glad to have someone to fill the empty seat at our table."

"I think you'll like it here," J.D. said suddenly, looking at her and speaking for the first time all period. "This place has a lot of stuff Ford didn't offer. The computers are better. Both the performing and visual arts programs are amazing for a high school. The libraries are much better than Ford's."

Amber nodded and smiled, once again her cheerful self. "I have picked up on a lot of that already," she said. "Lincoln's a good school. I'm looking forward to the year."

J.D. gave her a lop-sided half smile that didn't make his bright blue eyes appear any more cheerful than they ever did. He then promptly dropped his eyes to his food and seemed suddenly, strangely, lost to the world. This was standard for him, and the rest of us had gotten desensitized to it. Amber was sensitive, though. The sudden change in J.D.'s countenance did not escape her perception, and she gave him an open and concerned stare. He was too far out to even notice her attention. The rest of us did, and when she suddenly realized that, she seemed embarrassed and looked down at her own food for a moment.

Then she looked up. "So have all of you been in the same schools since kindergarten?" she asked. She obviously knew J.D. hadn't, but she also knew that J.D. wasn't participating in the conversation. The rest of us chattered lightly about this and that for a few minutes. Then J.D. finished his lunch, mumbled a goodbye, and left, and Amber watched him go. We'd just met her, but I knew she was getting an accurate vibe of our little group, and she was going to be part of it.

Chapter twenty-two ~

On Saturday, a couple weeks later, T.J. and I were alone in our house at 2:30 a.m. Boyne was spending the night with a friend. Mom had taken Shannon on a weekend to Boston, her gift for her eighth birthday a couple weeks before (not sure why, but eight is considered a milestone in my family). My dad had stayed home but gone in on a call from the hospital just before two, so it was just us. Or at least I thought it was. I was asleep, but I woke when I heard someone calling my name.

When I opened my eyes, I saw J.D. standing in the middle of my room, grinning at me around a red sucker in his mouth. He was bouncing up and down on the toes of his sock-clad feet and swinging his arms in every direction. His clothes were wrinkled, his hair was messed-up, and sweat was pouring off of his body as if he were running a marathon.

I thought I was dreaming. J.D. had never come into my room before, and he'd never really grinned; and while he had a tendency to talk with his mouth full, he'd never done aerobics with a lollipop clamped between his teeth. I doubted he would ever do any of those things, much less all three at the same time. But I yawned, which I didn't remember ever doing in a dream. It also struck me as strange, since yawning is highly contagious, that J.D. didn't yawn when he saw me do it. I sat up. "What are you doing?" I asked him, incredulously.

He was breathing heavily, but he didn't even take the sucker out of his mouth and couldn't seem to stop bouncing or swinging his arms. He answered me with the sucker stick clenched solidly between his teeth. "Nothing," he told me.

"How'd you get into my house?"

"The key under the yellow rosebush." He bounced forward, held out his hands, and showed me thorn scratches on the backs before promptly resuming the arrhythmic motion of his arms. Duh, I thought. I knew J.D. knew about the key, since I had been locked out one day when J.D. brought me home from school.

I frowned as he bounced backward a couple paces. His bouncing with the sucker in his mouth worried me. I know that sounds like an overly maternal reaction, but Boyne and Shannon are prone to actions similar to the ones J.D. was exhibiting at the time. "You should get rid of that thing before you trip and jam it down your throat," I told him.

He stared at me blankly for a moment before going into a fit of tight-lipped yet hysterical laughter.

"What?" I asked, slightly offended by his behavior.

"I can't," he told me.

"Huh?"

"I can't take it out." His laughter subsided slowly.

"What do you mean you can't take it out?"

"I can't open my mouth." He broke into a fresh fit of odd, hysterical laughter.

I stared at him then suddenly blurted, "You have lockjaw?"

He thought for a second, still bouncing and swinging his arms. "Yes," he said finally.

"Well, what's wrong? Are you feeling okay?"

"I feel great!" he told me.

"But-" I began, then it suddenly occurred to me. "What did you take?" I asked him urgently.

He laughed again, more subdued than before. "I honestly am not sure," he rejoined. "They put something on the candy at the club I was at tonight."

I couldn't believe it. "You didn't know what it was or what it could do to you, and you put it into your body? You didn't know…" I stopped talking, because I suddenly knew what it was. Increased metabolism. Euphoria. Lockjaw. A club. "Ecstasy," I told him.

"Huh?" By then he was jumping up, slapping his hands on my eight-foot ceiling.

"It was ecstasy."

"Oh. Cool."

"'Cool'? J.D., if you take too much of that, your heart explodes."

"That's okay."

I wanted to slap him. I even hopped out of my bed to do it, but I caught myself and crossed my arms over my chest. "It can give you chronic, terminal depression."

He gave me a "so-what's-new" look.

"Why did you come here?" I asked him.

"Closing time," he said. I guessed he was referring to the club where he'd gotten the ecstasy.

"But why here?" I asked.

"Why not?"

I sighed. "Okay. Why don't you go downstairs to the kitchen? I'll come down in a few minutes and make some coffee." J.D. jumped once more and slapped the ceiling. "Or herbal tea," I said.

He turned and exited my bedroom at a jog, and I hurried to get dressed, combed, and brushed so I could join him in the kitchen. He was still bouncing off the walls when I got to the kitchen, but he started coming down before four-thirty. It wasn't long before he was slumping in a chair at the kitchen table, staring into his mug with a dejected expression on his face, and wondering why I'd decided on herbal tea. "You can't convince it to become caffeinated by staring it down," I reminded. "You don't need caffeine now, anyway. You need to go home, take some Advil and a warm shower, and get a few hours of sleep."

He shrugged and said nothing. He looked more depressed than ever. I knew my dad would've said it was just that his "serotonin was depleted", but I wanted to cry, seeing him like that. "Why do you do this to yourself?" I asked him.

He gave me a look that scared me. It was the kind of look you'd give a person who'd broken into your house then pulled a "Saturday Night Special" on you when you confronted them, but you were holding a loaded double-barrel shotgun behind your back. "Why do you care what I do to myself?" he asked me.

"You're my friend," I told him. "I care about you."

"Well, don't. I don't care about you."

"J.D." I reached out to touch his arm, and he pushed back, throwing over his chair in the process.

"No!" he shouted. "Don't touch me. I'm stronger now. I'm not going to let you hurt me."

"I'm not trying to hurt you."

"Yes, you are. You are. You're just like everyone else. 'Better run! Tuck, duck, and roll!' All you want with me is to hurt me. That's all anybody wants with me. All you are is just like everyone else."

"No, J.D., I'm not," I said. "I'm not like everybody else! Those people who hurt you and used you and left you - those people have nothing to do with me! The last things I'd ever want would be to hurt or use you, and if I ever wanted to leave, you can bet I'd already be gone."

"Then I'll leave." He left the house, slamming the door behind him. I could practically hear my heart shatter on the floor when the Saturn pulled away.

"So, where are your motivational speaking skills now, Annie Eire?" I asked myself as I picked up the chair J.D. had knocked over. Those famed skills hadn't worked on J.D. that time. They never worked on J.D. They went on vacation to Europe to "find themselves" when J.D. was around. I frowned and dumped the mugs into the sink.

Why didn't my speaking skills work on J.D.? I knew the answer to that. It was because they weren't really mine. J.D. had told me to speak from my heart when I gave my talk during the retreat, but I hadn't; I'd spoken from God's heart. A lot of the time, when I spoke like that, I could just shut up and let God give me words to say. But it didn't always work that way, especially with J.D. For some reason I didn't understand, J.D. had the power to, with one despairing look or word, turn me into a panicked fool. When I was panicked, the words coming out of my mouth were from my heart, instead of God's, and my words didn't have the same power as those of the One who'd spoken the universe into existence.

Why had J.D. come to my house, anyway? What made him think of me, and the key under my mom's rosebush when he was higher than the moon? Why hadn't he gone to the beach, or a rest stop, someplace where he wouldn't be bothered? Of course he was scared of going home, but my place wasn't much different, especially since he wouldn't have known my parents weren't home, and he had to have known they'd call Jim if they found him.

I kind of thought he'd come to me wanting me to give him some sort of help, but he hadn't seemed like he wanted help of any sort when I'd tried to give him some. But why then? He'd said he wanted me to leave him alone. Why on earth would he come to my house, to my room, in the small hours of the morning if he wanted me to leave him alone? It didn't make sense.

By nine, I was exhausted, not only from the lack of sleep, but also from emotional stress and whirlwind thoughts. I knew it would be useless for me to try to get back to sleep. I was almost jealous of my little brother who'd slept through J.D.'s entire visit and hadn't woken still. I decided to go out to the picnic table in the backyard. I was hoping some fresh air would help clear my head, but nothing could blow J.D. out of my mind. He and his problems were stuck in my consciousness like bubble gum in shag carpeting. I hated the way he hurt, the pain he felt. I had to struggle against hating the people who'd hurt him, but I didn't even try not to hate what they did and the way they could just go on with their lives while J.D. had turned into a depressed, recreational drug user. They were fine while he couldn't endure a friendly handshake, and after the accident, he was cringing just as much from the touch of the doctors as from his broken ankle.

J.D. was my friend. I cared about him. I loved him, even. The fact that he was hurting hurt me. My friends had always been having problems, but that past year had been totally over-stocked in the problems department, and worse things had happened than had ever happened before. The issues with J.D. were the worst of them all. Ben's brother had committed suicide, but Ben was dealing with it, and Ben had God. J.D. didn't have God, and J.D. wasn't dealing with any of the things that had happened to him. He was dying inside and rotting away, even though he wasn't quite dead. He was experiencing pain beyond my comprehension, and the fact that I couldn't understand or empathize with it only made me feel worse.

As I sat at the picnic table in my backyard, I started to realize I was almost choking myself to hold back my tears. I took a deep but broken breath and looked around. The mid-morning/late summer sun was shining brightly. The late roses and chrysanthemums were blooming all around me in the garden. The birds were singing. It was a beautiful day, but that didn't make me feel better, except to help me realize I had no reason not to cry. So I let go and cried. But I didn't simply cry. I wept, and I prayed in broken and mixed-up sentences. I was too upset to put together clear thoughts; but, you know, I think God can understand whatever it is you can manage to say at the time.

And bless Him for that, because I sat on that table crying for more than a half hour. It was almost ten o'clock when I felt comforting arms wrap around my shoulders from behind and a kiss land warmly on the top of my head. Daddy…I thought, and for a brief second wondered how the surgery had gone. When that thought disappeared, it was replaced by a clear sense of resolution, and my tears and sobs trailed away. "It's okay," I said. "I feel better now. Thanks, Daddy."

"Um…no," I heard. It wasn't my Dad. The arms released me, and I swung my legs over the picnic bench, turned, stood up, and stared at J.D.

"You…" I began but couldn't finish.

"Yeah…me…what?" He was grinning, but I didn't worry.

"You touched me." I was shocked.

"Yeah, it's kinda nice, huh?" he said and pulled me into his arms before I could say anything. After a few seconds, he let me go, stepped back, and offered me his right hand. I shook it. "Nice to meet you," he said.

I giggled, and he hugged me again. "I'm sorry," he said into my hair. "I'm so sorry. I know you don't want to hurt me, and I know you care about me, and we're friends, and I care about you, too." He let me go.

"Thanks," I told him. "But what happened this morning?"

"Nothing happened. Not this morning. Two millennia ago. Jesus happened. I just recognized it. You were right this whole time, Aine, and I'm glad I figured it out before it was too late."

"Wow," I said. Now that half a million of my prayers had been answered, I was in shock. "That's great, J.D. I've been praying for that since you fell out of the ceiling last November."

He smiled (that in itself was amazing). "I know."

I smiled, too. "This is so great. Oh!" I exclaimed, suddenly. "We should go tell everyone! That would be good." My voice dropped to just above a whisper. "You could shake their hands – they'd like that. Did you give your parents hugs?"

"Yeah, I did. They liked that. I did, too. Let's go."

Chapter twenty-three ~

Mom and Shannon were glad to hear about J.D., too. Mom gave J.D. a motherly hug, and Shannon sat on his lap while she told us about her weekend. "We went to see the Tea Party Boat and the museum and the Lex…Lex…What was it called, Mommy?"

"Lexington Green," my mother supplied.

"Yeah, that. We saw tons of stuff. We learned all about the Revolutionary War."

"That's exciting," I told her.

"Yes," she agreed. "The hotel was neat, too."

"What hotel was that?" I asked.

"O'Reilly's Inn and Suites," Mom told me.

"They have a pool," Shannon said. "And a game room, and a snack bar called Finn MacCool's, and a gift shop, and a fancy restaurant. I made a new little friend."

"You did?"

"Yeah, and she's only four." Shannon, being the youngest of four, likes having a friend or two who are younger than she.

"The owner of O'Reilly's, Jonathan Kavanagh-" Mom began.

"Kavanagh?" I quizzed. "Not O'Reilly?"

"O'Reilly was his wife's maiden name. Anyway, Mr. Kavanagh lives on the fourth floor of the hotel with his granddaughter. They have adjoining rooms with a living room and a kitchenette attached; it's a nice set up. We met the little girl, and she's a real sweetheart. She and Shannon really hit it off."

"She's fun," Shannon said.

"Yes, and as cute as a button. Blue eyes, strawberry blonde hair, little upturned nose, and an adorable Boston accent. And wonderful manners for such a little person."

"You sound like you wanted to bring her home," I commented.

"Maybe I did, a little," Mom admitted, reluctantly.

"What's your friend's name?" I asked Shannon.

"Crea," she answered. (Pronounced "Cree").

"From the Gaelic 'Croi,' right?" I asked Mom. "Heart."

"It's actually her middle name. Her first name is Catriona." (Pronounced like 'Katrina').

I smiled. "Pure heart. A great name."

Mom nodded and explained, "Mr. Kavanagh named her."

I smiled and looked at Shannon. "So tell me about your visit to Boston Harbor," I said.

She gave me a blank look, and I amended, "The Tea Party Boat."

"Oh, that." Her eyes lit up. "They told us about how they dressed up like Indians and made tea in the water 'round the boat."

"Made tea in the water?" I questioned dubiously.

"Well, you make tea by putting it in water, right?"

I smiled, and J.D. leaned his chin on the top of her little red head. "Did you learn why they threw the tea into the harbor?" I asked.

"'Cause the English put a tax on the tea."

"Do you know why the colonists didn't like the tax?"

"'Cause they didn't have a Senator."

J.D. grinned at her answer, and I giggled. "Close enough," I told her. She smiled proudly, satisfied with that. "Now, tell us what happened on Lexington Green."

Her eyes lit up again as she launched into another explanation. Shannon loves explaining things she's learned, and anyone who has ever heard her explain anything loves to hear it. Her excitement is inspiring. She's also like the little girl from the Boston inn: so cute.

Then there's Vanessa Montgomery. Cute? Not so much. She thought it was really cute at the time. My friends and I weren't amused. The first day we went back to school after J.D.'s transformation, someone happened to mention to me during my second hour class that they'd heard something about "that guy I hung out with."

"Who?" I asked them.

"The blond guy."

"J.D.?"

"Yeah."

"What about him?"

"I heard he's in foster care 'cause his mom's a junkie and his dad's in prison for murder."

I laughed - in disbelief, not amusement - and asked, "Where on earth did you hear that?" I finally chased it back to guess who. Mark heard the rumor, too, and between fourth hour and lunch, we were talking about how we should confront Vanessa.

"Maybe Adam could talk to her," Mark suggested.

"They broke up last year."

"I know that, but I'm not so clueless I can't tell she still likes him. He's got leverage."

"He wouldn't take advantage of that, though. He's not the person to be our hatchet man."

"You're right"

"I say we just kill her."

"Relax, kid."

"But, Mark…" I seethed. "Man. She's just never gonna learn."

"That takes time, Annie. You know that."

"But how could she start-" Mark suddenly raised his eyebrows and shook his head almost imperceptibly. We've been friends long enough to know each other's signals. I stopped, turned around, and said, "Hi, J.D."

"Hey, Aine. Mark." We stood in the hallway in awkward silence for a moment. J.D. finally shattered it. "I've heard the rumor, guys," he said.

Mark and I watched him, waiting.

"It's funny these people think they know me better than I know myself," he continued.

Mark shrugged. I wrinkled the bridge of my nose and gave J.D. a lopsided smile. He sighed deeply. "It was Vanessa Montgomery, right?" he asked.

I nodded.

"I should go talk to her."

I shrugged.

"Annie, I hate to ask you this, but will you come with me?"

I frowned, solemnly. "Yeah. Okay."

We tracked Vanessa down after school, outside the gym before cheerleading practice. "Miss Montgomery," J.D. greeted as we walked up behind her.

She turned. "Oh, hi...um..." she faltered. "...Mr. Foster."

"J.D. Please. You seem to know me quite well, after all."

"Yeah, well, um…"

"Actually better than I know myself, it would seem," he continued.

She didn't respond. She already felt badly about the rumor she'd started; perhaps she felt badly even before J.D. confronted her.

"Why?" J.D. asked her. "Have I done something to you I'm not aware of? I mean, if I've done something, fine; I'm sorry. But tell me about it, I just don't understand…" His voice died off, and I frowned. The only thing he'd done was not be as interested in her as she was in herself. Vanessa sighed and thought for a minute, looking slightly ashamed.

"Nothing really. I was…just having a little…fun."

J.D. snorted. "Fun?"

"Yeah, well…Look, I'm sorry if your friends…"

He interrupted her, "My friends' opinions of me aren't influenced by that type of information, true or false. That's not what bothers me."

"What does, then?"

"That, you wouldn't understand." He turned to go, and I got ready to leave with him.

"Hey, um, J.D.?" Vanessa called after him.

He turned back.

"Why are you in foster care?" J.D. looked at her but said nothing. She continued, "If you don't want to tell me…"

"It's not that. I don't mind. I just don't know, and I hate that. That's why rumors like that bother me. I don't know, and I know no one else does. If anyone finds anything out for real, I'd love to know. I'd want to be the first to know."

"I'm sorry," she said, frowning. "I'm a jerk. I'm supposed to be getting better at this."

He shrugged and gave her an encouraging smile. "It takes time, you know," he said.

"But, look at you. I've heard about you. You're totally different already."

"Not everything is visible, Vanessa. And not everything is so easy."

He turned again, and we headed for my car.

"I drew ya something," he told me as we walked out the side door of the school building.

"In art class?" I asked.

"Yeah." We stopped while J.D. pulled a piece of laminated paper out of his pack and handed it to me. I examined it. On the front, the paper boasted a leprechaun standing in an emerald green landscape. The little elf was holding out his hand in a "come on" gesture, and written in gold, gothic lettering against the background over his head were the words, "Welcome to Aine's Little Ireland."

"This is cool," I told J.D.

"Turn it over," he told me. On the back of the page, a midnight blue sky shone with gold stars, a pearly white moon, and silver lettering that said, "Shh! Annie is sleeping…Regularly scheduled tours will resume in the morning."

I shook my head, smiled, and looked up at J.D. "I thought you were too stoned to notice the little theme I had going," I observed.

He shrugged. "Not quite," he said. "But it is pretty obvious, you have to admit."

Well, sure. By "Aine's Little Ireland," J.D. was referring to my bedroom. It's obvious I'm interested in Ireland. Everything in my bedroom is either emerald green or a shamrock print. My bookshelves are stocked with books about Ireland, set in Ireland, penned by Irish authors, or written in Irish Gaelic. I have green linens, toys and mini-blinds. My walls hold maps and pictures of Ireland and a green souvenir plaque with gold lettering that says, "O'Brien's Pub." My ceiling is a gigantic collage of Ireland maps, posters, post cards, pictures, drawings, and everything else Ireland. "Wow!" I said, suddenly, as we started walking again. "This would make a good website. You know, about Ireland."

J.D. thought for a second and nodded. "Yeah," he said. "That would be cool."

"This picture could be on the main page, and we could put links on it, like traditions, history, legends and folklore, and a Gaelic dictionary."

"An atlas would be good. And Irish food. Mark could help. We could pull together an awesome site."

"You think so?"

"Forget mall shoe store associates. We'd be bona fide website designers."

"Well, I don't know if we could make a job out if it."

"Sure, we could."

I giggled at the idea, but he might've been serious.

Chapter twenty-four ~

The next day I found out what had been going on with Juliana since February. I went to her house after school, because I hoped we could hang out, girls only. We hadn't in a while, and I thought it was long overdue. Her mom answered the door and showed me up to her room. When I walked into Juli's room, I noticed the packed suitcases right away, but I decided to give her some time to bring them up herself. I told her about the website and asked if she'd like to come over to Mark's sometime and lend us her creative genius. She pulled a J.D. on me, a shrug and a "Sure, whatever."

"How about this weekend?" I suggested.

"I'm busy."

"Doing what?"

She didn't answer. The suspense was killing me, so I asked, "Where you going?"

"Nowhere."

"No fair lying, Juliana." I sat down next to her on the floor.

"Annie-"

"Come on, Juli."

"I'm going to California. I'm leaving tomorrow."

"What? Leaving?"

"I'm coming back. I'll miss tomorrow and Friday at school, fly back on Monday and be back in class on Tuesday morning."

"Does Ben know?"

"I couldn't tell him."

"Why not?"

"'Cause he would've asked me the question you're about to ask me."

"Yeah, like, why are you going out to California in the middle of the school year?"

She sighed, pursed her lips, and shrugged.

"Juli…Come on…You've been keeping secrets way too long."

"Not 'secrets'. Only one."

"It's still the same thing?"

"Yeah."

"So…why? You can unload on me; I can take it."

"You've always been a good person to vent to. No miracles, you just listen and say the perfect thing if such a thing exists."

"It's my gift. So share the baggage already."

She frowned, pulled her knees up to her chest, and said, "I've no idea where to start."

"Well, how about starting with why you're going to California?"

"I'm going to California to visit my dad."

I stared at her in confusion. "What?" I asked.

"Because that's where he lives now, in Huntington Beach."

I had no idea her father lived anywhere but in that house. "Since when?"

"Since about a month-and-a-half ago." I continued staring dumbly. I wasn't feeling very motivating. She went on, "Mom kicked Dad out that day you and J.D. found me on the sidewalk. The divorce was finalized about a week-and-a-half ago, but Dad got a job there about six weeks ago and has been living on the beach."

I never would've expected that. Juli looked at me. "Yeah, I know," she said. "When I found out, I was more shocked than you are now."

That has been one thing I've noticed. Kids rarely expect their parents to get divorced. Parents think the kids must know something terrible is going on, but kids usually assume what they experience at home is normal. Ceara, my dad's older sister, got divorced about six years ago, and Ingrid and her brother Liam were utterly blown out of the water by it. Divorce rocks a kid's world, and parents just don't get that. Juliana's eyes were beginning to tear. I squeezed her shoulder.

"Why didn't you tell us about it before? Why couldn't you at least tell Ben?"

"My mom just kept giving me that, 'Remember-no-one-needs-to-know-our-personal-business' speech. But she won't even talk to me about it, and it makes my Dad uncomfortable to talk about it. I didn't have any place to turn. You can only keep this kind of thing inside of yourself for so long."

"I know. Hey, you still get to see your dad, though. Maybe not as much as before…But Surf City, USA. That's cool."

Juli sniffled and giggled softly. "I've never been to Huntington Beach before."

"You should talk to Ben about this. He's been concerned, and he's felt like you're pushing him away. I think if you tell your mom that, she'll come back to earth and see what's more important."

"You're probably right. We haven't really talked about how isolated I feel and how you guys, especially Ben, feel shut out."

"Then do it. Plus, she's isolating herself in her pain, too. It'll help her to let some out."

"You're right."

"I'll be heading home, then, so you can get to it. I'll see you. And enjoy your trip."

"I will. I'm starting to feel better. Thanks for being pushy this time."

She gave me a hug. I smiled. "Oh," I said. "It's just 'The Great Motivator' at work."

She giggled. "See ya, Annie Eire."

*****

My friends and I waited until Juli got back, then got together and built an awesome website. We didn't do any advertising, so it was cool that it had gotten a hundred hits by the time it was open a week.

In November, Mark showed "Aine's Little Ireland" to the owner of State Street Joe's, and he hired us to build the coffee shop's new site. Mark and Amber put together a DBA for our company, Flames & Gold, Incorporated, and we built a marketing site for FnGI with "portfolio" links to State Street Joe's and Aine's Little Ireland. I began to think maybe J.D. had been right about us becoming web designers.

He was also right about one part of our website: we Irish aren't known for our fancy cooking, but the Irish cuisine page was the most popular part of Little Ireland.

Chapter twenty-five-

J.D. and I had speech class together, and in late November the teacher had asked us to prepare a presentation of a story or a couple poems that we could give in front of a group of elementary kids. The teacher told us she was going to pick her two favorite presentations from each of her speech classes to show to the lower classes at the nearest elementary school. J.D. and I had teamed up and, with Shannon's help, picked two poems by A. A. Milne, called "Sneezles" and "Vespers". Milne wrote both of the poems about his son Christopher Robin, and J.D. and I rigged up a sort of choral reading for each of them. J.D. drew up the visual aids, and I colored them. It worked out well. Ours was one of the ones the teacher chose.

The day before Thanksgiving was the day we went to Jefferson Elementary. Apparently, the elementary school speech outing was a big deal, because it got us out of the whole day of school. The teacher had given each group a schedule during class the day before, and told us we could stay in the teacher's lounge when we weren't presenting.

We boarded the bus as soon as we got to school that morning. A dark-haired boy and a blonde girl were already on the bus, and while J.D. and I were passing them, the boy gave a J.D. a dirty look. J.D. gave him a friendly, almost apologetic smile, and kept walking. Once we were seated, I looked at J.D. with the question on my face. "Someone from Ford," he murmured. "We'll talk later."

I nodded, and our chance to talk came during our first break in the teacher's lounge at Jefferson. A couple guys who were doing one of the stories from <u>Arabian Nights</u> were also on break, but they were engrossed in a euchre game. I only gave J.D. a curious look, and he started telling me. "It's not much of a story," he said. "His name is Matthew Cox. We knew each other at Ford, actually before, in junior high. He lived across the street from the Bauers. We were mortal enemies."

"Did he give you a hard time about your family or something?"

"You give me too much credit, Aine. It was mostly me. I mean, he knocked me around a little, but I started it. It was cheap. I was having a bad day, and I sucker-punched him in the hall for no reason."

"Why him?"

"I was jealous."

"What of?"

"His life. He had everything I wanted. Nothing extravagant, you know. Just status quo. Middle class. He had an older brother, a younger sister, and a dog. Family had a normal house in the suburbs. His parents were in the PTA. His mom chaperoned field trips and made cookies for the band bake sale. His dad played football with him and his brother in their front yard. His sister was in the Brownies. He had a paper route, and his brother worked in the mall. I hated that he had the life I wanted, while I was stuck with the mess I had. I was a complete jerk; he eventually decided he wasn't gonna let me bully him anymore, and by the time I left Ford, no one else could remember who'd started it."

*****

J.D. and I delivered our presentation to the third graders before lunch. It was well-received, but my little sister was undoubtedly our biggest fan in the room. The whole group of us went to McDonald's for lunch, and when J.D. and I returned to the teacher's lounge, we found Matthew Cox and his blonde partner there. J.D. and I sat down at a table near the couch where Matthew and the girl were sitting. Nobody said anything for a while before J.D. said, "Hey, Matt."

Matt didn't say anything, just stared at my friend. J.D. stood, walked over to him, and said, "Hey, I'm sorry for being such a jerk when we were neighbors. We could've been friends, but I was stupid, and I regret it. Forgive me?"

J.D. offered his right hand, and Matt stared at him for another minute before nodding and offering his own. "I was wondering where you'd ended up after you disappeared a year ago, Foster," he said.

"Yeah," J.D. said, smiling again. "Here I am. Lincoln High."

"Well, it's been good for you."

"What do you mean?"

"I don't know. It's in your eyes, I guess. You're different somehow. So different, you're almost hard to recognize."

"Oh," J.D. said. "Different, sure. But it's not Lincoln. Lincoln is a disaster for me; I'd broken every social rule within the first week. I only got one reason I'm still breathing."

"And what is that? If you don't mind me asking." Matthew might've been needling J.D. with his tone, but J.D. wasn't gonna take the bait on that...further evidence that there was something to what he was talking about.

"Not at all," J.D. said. "Do you believe in God?"

Matt was a little surprised at the question. "I don't know. What? Are you gonna try to proselytize me?"

"I don't know what that means," J.D. told him, "but I would like to tell you...the meaning of life."

"Oh, right. Do tell."

I just sat in my chair, trying not to grin.

My friends and I worked on a few more websites in December, and January brought more business, which was exciting.

January also brought a new semester with many new classes. Amber and I found ourselves in second hour senior composition together. The first project we had in senior comp. was an opinion paper. The teacher, who had been teaching composition for years and become bored reading the same papers, had offered extra credit points for obscure topics. I opted to write a slightly humorous paper called "Rap: Is It Music?" Amber chose to write about business ethics.

During the first day of research, Kevin Sheridan, the kid whose face J.D. had once pinned to the hood of a Miata, started teasing Amber about her topic. Strangely, that teasing quickly turned into a full-scale debate about right and wrong and God. Kevin was an atheist. Or rather, he claimed to be while Amber stated that he probably wasn't. Amber said that when it came down to it, few people could be atheists. Without God, who makes the rules? To be an atheist was to believe in a world entirely without right and wrong, because there was no One to decide.

"Right and wrong is subjective," Kevin said. "What you believe is wrong for you may not be wrong for me. I may not believe in it."

"Truth does not rely on belief," Amber countered. "Not believing something doesn't make it untrue, and believing something doesn't make it true. I could believe with every ounce of my soul that I could fly, but if I jumped from the observation deck of the Empire State Building, my body would have a quick and uncomfortable meeting with the ground."

"But physics and morality are two entirely different things," Kevin argued. "And I still don't see what any of this has to do with God."

"Morality is directly related to God, because God decides morality. If you believe in morality at all, you have to believe in God. If God doesn't exist, who makes the rules?"

"But that's what I was saying. Rules are social constructs. Morality is subjective."

"That's an intellectually dishonest point of view."

"What do you mean?"

"Well, merely to say, 'There is no absolute morality' is a contradiction, because 'no' itself is an absolute. The statement denies absolutes, but makes an absolute declaration concerning morality; it's just not logical."

"Well, morals aren't logical. They're emotional."

"I could argue the inaccuracy of that statement, but even if it were accurate, a true denial of absolute morals would require a point of view completely devoid of human emotion."

"What?"

"The best way to illustrate that would be to play a rather graphic game of make-believe."

"Okay. Whatever. Shoot."

"I think I will. In fact, let's close our eyes and pretend we live in a world without God."

"But we do."

"Well, if you believe that, you won't have trouble pretending. In this world without God, I brought a couple of high-caliber, semi-automatic handguns and a smaller caliber weapon to school today, and I brought them to this library where we are sitting right now, during this class. Right now, I pulled them out of my bag, shot, and killed everyone in this room except for you and me. I don't kill you; I pop one of the smaller rounds into your stomach, so you're dying slowly, bleeding to death inside your own body.

"Now, I have my cell phone here. I could make a call, and in minutes, you'd be on your way to the hospital where you'd get the care that would save your life. But I don't use the phone; I hold a gun on you instead. You call out, and your best friend, who's walking by the library at that moment, comes to help. I shoot and kill your friend. No one else is coming – if they do, they die. I have your death in my hands and your life in my jacket pocket. What are you going to tell me, Kevin? What are you going to say as you beg for your life?"

"Well, I'd say, if you let me die, they'll put you in prison."

"Come on, Kevin. I've just killed more than thirty people. They're gonna put me in prison anyway, probably for the rest of my life. You have to make me believe that saving your life is the right thing to do."

"It is. Killing me is against the law."

"Says who? Who makes the rules, Kevin?"

"Says me. Says everyone."

"I don't. I say killing you is the right thing to do. I know other people out there somewhere wouldn't mind letting you die, either. What makes your opinion or anyone else's better than mine?"

"Well, judges say it's wrong to kill me."

"So? What's so special about judges? They're all just people, and I'm a person, too. What makes them better than me?"

Kevin was stuck for a minute, but then he rejoined with, "But what about my family and my friends?"

"What about your family and your friends?"

"They'll miss me."

"All of these people's families and friends will miss them, too. All the more reason to kill you. To make it fair for everyone's families and friends. You need to give me a real reason. Your time is running out."

"But we could go on like this forever."

195

"Exactly. We could. But in a world with God, it's easier. In a world with God, the only answer necessary for that question is, 'It's wrong because God said it's wrong.' And, honestly, Kevin, which world makes more sense, logically *and* emotionally? A world where there is nothing saying a person shouldn't run around randomly killing others? Or a world where it's wrong because a presiding Authority dictates just that?"

Chapter twenty-six ~

One day in mid-February, my friends and I preempted movie night to go to a real movie. We decided to go to a nine-thirty show, but we went to the theatre at seven-thirty because the guys wanted to play some of the arcade games. We girls thought about letting the guys go on ahead and coming later, but the best car pool deal was for Mark, J.D., and me to ride together and Ben, Juli, and Amber to ride together. When J.D., Mark, and I arrived, Ben was already in the arcade, and Juliana and Amber were sitting at a table in the atrium, eating chocolate-covered raisins. J.D. and Mark came with me to the table to say hello (and to get some raisins). Juliana offered some candy, which we all took.

"Hey, you guys could get some food while we're here," J.D. suggested. Even though Jay Dillon felt pretty secure about not being starved again (especially since the Jacobses had kept him on after his supposed eighteenth birthday), he was still quite preoccupied with food.

"Ooo..." Juli said.

I grinned, and Juliana and I both stood up to head toward the concession stand. Amber nibbled on another of Juli's raisins. J.D. watched her and cocked his blond head slightly to the left. "What about you?" Mark asked her.

She shrugged. J.D. shrugged at her, sat down on the table (yes, on – not at), and said to her, "See, Amber, one thing I've learned is you can't get away with shrugs in this group. I should know, because these people call shrugging, 'pulling a J.D.'"

She smiled. "I could barely pull off buying the ticket, and I-"

"Is that all?" Mark asked. "Look, I'll buy you some food."

"That's okay, Mark."

"Come on, Amber. Let the over-privileged computer geek share the wealth."

She sighed and smiled. "All right. Thank you, Mark."

"My pleasure." Mark followed us to the concession stand and bought Amber a pretzel with cheese, gummy bears, and a Dr. Pepper. After paying for Amber's food, Mark headed to the arcade while Juli and Amber headed back to the table. I detoured slightly to walk with Mark.

"Next time," I advised him, "buy her ticket too."

"What?"

"Mark, when are you gonna ask her out?"

"Annie!"

"But, Mark, we'd all endorse this. She's much better than the other three girls you've dated. You two connect; it's like you're the only person who doesn't see it."

"I see it, Annie. I see Amber. It's just..."

"She likes you, too. She wouldn't let anyone else buy her food. We all know that, and we all know she thinks you're special. She always has."

"Maybe," he conceded.

"So ask her. I have to get back, but think about it."

I went back to the table and sat down with the other girls, and we prayed together before beginning to eat. We chatted while we ate, and Amber was finishing a joke when I felt a gentle tug on a lock of my hair, and a hand reached over my shoulder to snag a few of my nachos. I turned around to look at J.D. munching on my food. "Hey," I said.

He chewed and swallowed before saying, "Thanks."

"Yeah, whatever. Do you need anything?"

"I want you to come play a game with me."

"You want?" I asked. Hey, he had asked me to help him with his manners.

"Please come play a game with me, Annie," he amended.

"Much better."

"So you'll play."

I shook my head. "I don't know how," I told him.

199

"I'll teach you," he offered, quickly.

"J.D…" I moaned.

"Please." He grabbed my right hand and tugged gently. He was playing with me, acting like a lonely, lost puppy to get what he wanted. It would have been cruel of him, if he didn't know that I knew exactly what he was doing. It wasn't working. Then he gave me this sweet, innocent smile, and those beautiful baby blues of his got really wide, and I figured, "Hey, I could play a video game to make my friend happy. It's just a video game."

"Okay, fine," I conceded.

He grinned. "Thanks, Annie." I followed him into the arcade, and he had me stand in front of the game – he stood behind me, reached around to the console, and began to explain. "It's a fighting game, and you try to beat-up the other guy on the screen. That," he said as he pointed to a green bar at the top of the screen, "is his life meter. The one on the other side of the screen is yours. You want to run his down before he runs yours down. This button is a kick, this is a punch…" He explained the game to me and was about to put the quarters in, but I stopped him.

"I don't think I can remember that," I told him. "What the buttons do, I mean."

"Okay, we'll play one game against the computer, and I'll help you." He put a quarter into the slot and put his hands over mine, using his fingers to guide mine to the right controls. He kept up an explanation monologue while he helped me play. "See, this is how you hit him. This lets you jump in the air and kick him in the head. This is just a regular kick…"

His head was bent down beside mine as he peered at the screen, and his voice was soft because his mouth was right beside my ear. I could feel his chest against my back and his arms brushing against mine as he guided my fingers. I don't think he'd ever been that close before, and it felt kind of weird – not bad, just weird. We knocked out a couple of people before losing, and J.D. put in enough quarters that we could play against each other.

I got confused on the controls and lost miserably in a matter of seconds, and J.D. felt the need to go through the entire explanation process again. All that work yielded the same results, and we went through the whole thing again. After the fourth time that he beat me to a bloody pulp before I was able to land a single punch, I got frustrated. He came over again, and started the tutorial thing all over. "Look," I told him, pushing back away from the machine, shoving him away in the process. "Why don't you just have Ben or Mark play? I've already wasted a fortune of quarters, and I don't want to play with you anymore. This is just not my thing."

He made eye contact with me, and he looked genuinely hurt. He choked out the word, "Fine," before turning and walking right out of the arcade. Ben, who'd been playing the game next to us, looked up and watched him go.

"What was the hairy conniption fit all about?" I asked him, exasperated.

"Annie," he said gently, "did it ever occur to you maybe J.D. just wants to spend time with you? That he just wants you around?" It hadn't. I looked down. "Look," Ben continued. "J.D.'s sort of socially inept, you know. And, emotionally, well, he's better than before, but...Most of the time, he doesn't understand a lot of what he feels. But he likes being around you."

"Are you saying he has a crush on me?"

"I don't know. He doesn't make a whole lot of sense to me; you understand him better than anyone else. All I'm saying is, if he did have a crush on you, he might not be able to categorize those feelings; and if he could categorize them, he would deny them with every ounce of will he possessed. Except he can't deny that he likes being around you."

"But why would he try to smother his feelings like that?"

"Because J.D. thinks...Well, it's like he feels the people who abused him... like, infected him somehow. Like he's carrying a virus, not physically, but...it's hard to explain. He's afraid if he gets close enough to someone like that, he'll pass his problems on to them, like a disease or something."

"How do you know this?"

"Well, we're guys. We talk about girls, and he's made comments like, 'I don't need a girlfriend. No reason to pass on the pollution.' Stuff like that."

"Why wouldn't he talk to me about any of this?"

"Aine, I'm going to give you a quiz," Ben said, "because while you understand Jay Dillon better than anyone else, you also seem blind to some of the fundamental elements of his character. For half a million dollars, let's just say, J.D. was experiencing a crush, and he was going to tell someone. Who, out of all the people he knows, would be the person most likely to understand him?"

"I guess me," I admitted.

"Right. And no 'I guess' about it. You're the only person in the world who can translate his nonsensical babble into something resembling plain English. But here's the million-dollar question. A paradox: if that crush was perhaps on you, Annie Eire, who, considering that whole 'damaged goods' delusion he has about himself, would be the person he'd be least likely to tell?"

I frowned, not wanting to admit it. "Also me," I murmured.

Ben awarded me with some lazy, limp-handed applause. "Ding! Ding! Ding!"

I looked down at my shoes, and Ben fell silent. After a few seconds of pause, adroitly inserted to spare my feelings, he continued, "And, in the words of Hamlet, 'Ay! There's the rub.' Now, if you'll excuse me, movie night would be a real drag if J.D.

got banned from the theater for ripping the soap dispensers off the wall in the men's bathroom." Ben leaned in close and went on in a mock-confidential tone, "He's a good kid; he just don't know what to do with all that frustration." He turned and headed off.

"I want my million dollars," I muttered as I watched him go. Even though he'd spoken as politely as he knew how, Ben left me feeling miserable. I'd never even considered J.D. might be harboring feelings like that. As for myself, well, I wasn't sure. I mean, I thought J.D. was cute, and I could get utterly and completely lost in his bright, blue eyes. He was also an intelligent guy with a good sense of humor and a great personality, and I did like being around him. I just felt incredibly stupid because I couldn't play a simple video game. And why did that matter? Because, I admitted to myself, out of everyone I knew, what Jay Dillon thought of me was the important thing.

Okay, so I wasn't exactly a pro at the whole boyfriend/girlfriend thing, either. I mean, I'd gone out on a couple dates two years before with this really nice guy from my church named Doug, but he'd moved to Maine, and that had been that. I'd invested most of my time in my friendships, not that that was a bad thing. But here I was, realizing it was entirely possible I was developing a crush on one of my friends who possibly had a crush on me, but probably had definite qualms about expressing his feelings - severe qualms, the kind that wouldn't be cleared up by a little push like the one I'd given Mark.

Ben came back into the arcade and gave me a thumbs-up. "All soap and paper dispensers are intact. His temper is improving."

"What did he say?"

"He muttered something about having gotten too close anyway. Look, I went in to stop him from damaging property, not to have girl-talk."

"Thanks, anyway." I frowned. "I should talk to him."

Ben shrugged. "He should be back soon."

J.D. came into the arcade a minute later, and I dragged him off to the side. "I'm sorry," I told him. "That was rude. I wasn't catching on, and I felt like an idiot."

He suddenly looked apologetic. "I'm sorry, Aine," he said. "I didn't mean to make you feel bad. That's not why I asked you to play."

"I know. It's not your fault. It's me. I just don't want to flaunt my shortcomings in front of you, and I need to learn to take bruises to my ego with more grace."

"You don't need to show off in front of me. We're not in competition."

I sighed. "It's not that. I just don't want you to think I'm incompetent or something."

His brow furrowed in confusion, then his eyes widened suddenly. He was probably thinking, "So it's some new, bizarre, perhaps PMS-laced, form of quasi-flirting?" "Aine," he said, "that would never cross my mind. You're awesome the way you are. I mean you design websites and improve the lives of almost every kid at our school. The game is not a big deal. I just wanted to hang out with you."

"Yeah. I figured that out a little late."

"It's okay. You're forgiven." I reached out to give him a hug, and he responded in kind, squeezing me tightly for a brief second before letting go. As he backed up, he gave me his I'd-like-to-thank-the-academy smile before looking down to check his watch.

"What time is it?" I asked.

He shrugged. "Eight twenty-four. We've still got quite a bit of time."

I gave him a half smile, glanced sideways at the game console, and said, "You want to try one more time?"

"If you don't mind…"

"I don't."

"Come on."

I was sort of getting the hang of it by the time we left the arcade. I'd never win any awards at it, but for his sake I was glad I'd tried.

Mark called me the next Wednesday night. "The checks from the Baptist Church and Wave Time Marine Supply both came today. Both are now paid in full for their completed websites, so I've just uploaded the last files onto their respective servers and sent them the access information."

"Great," I said. "Make sure Amber knows the money came." Amber handled the bookkeeping and legal aspects of FnGI, because she was the best at that sort of thing. She was so good at it that she had decided to go to college for business administration. She had, strangely enough, already been accepted to same university that Mark was attending for some complicated computer degree I didn't really understand. They'd applied to the same school each without knowing about the other's application. I'd wondered aloud to Mark several times if that had any deep significance.

"She does," he was telling me now. "She's already prepared the deposit for tomorrow and printed our wage checks for those two sites and for The Coffee Stop money we got early in the week. She's post-dated them for Monday to give the deposit a chance to clear, but I thought you guys could come over to collect your checks and celebrate the completion of three incredible websites."

"Sounds good…So Amber's at your house already?"

"Yeah, we were just coming here from a coffee date when we found the checks."

"Ooo…Coffee date…" I admit it, I was gushing just a little.

"Annie, please don't…" He was embarrassed.

"I'm proud of you."

"Yeah, yeah. Anyway, I gotta call everyone else, so…"

"I'll be over in a minute."

I grabbed a couple bottles of sparkling grape juice for a celebration toast (three amazing websites were one thing, but Mark and Amber's first date deserved something special) and hopped next door. Fifteen minutes later, everyone had their glass raised while we recited reasons to celebrate. I looked at J.D. and noticed he had already drained half his glass. I giggled and took it from him for a refill. "You're supposed to wait to drink until after we say, 'Cheers,'" I told him.

"Yeah?" he asked.

I nodded, supposing it was quite possible with the places he'd lived that he hadn't been exposed to many toasts.

"I won't do it again," he said. "But I wanted to make a toast too, because I'm celebrating."

"Cool," Ben said. "What's up?"

"I got my college acceptance."

"Congratulations!" Amber chirped and hurried to give him a quick hug. The rest of us followed to offer our best wishes. J.D. had been a little behind the rest of us with his college applications (at Lincoln, they give you a college prep calendar in seventh grade), so he was the last to hear back.

"Where are you going?" Juli asked.

"University of Massachusetts at Boston," he said.

I felt my eyes widening in surprise.

"Aine," J.D. continued, "I know that's where you're going, but I'm not stalking you. I didn't know it was your top choice when I applied. Mostly I just liked the idea of going to Boston."

"Well, Boston's a nice city," I told him, "and I'm glad we'll be at the same school. It'll be good to have someone there that I know."

He nodded. "I'm glad you'll be there, too," he told me.

"Anyway," Amber said, raising her glass, "cheers to all of that and to everything else we can't think of right now." She used her free hand to grab Mark's.

"Slainte!" I said, and J.D. smiled at my use of the Irish.

Everyone echoed the toast and clinked glasses. As I took my first sip, I noticed Mark giving me a meaningfully look, then glancing sideways at J.D. He was making the same hints about J.D. and I going to the same school that I'd made about he and Amber; I gave him my best teasing glare. Still, I couldn't help wondering a little.

Chapter twenty-seven ~

My family usually goes someplace amazing for spring break. Of course, we hadn't gone anywhere when I was small and Dad had med school and student loans. When I was older, we'd gone to the Bahamas, New York City, Ireland, and other places.

This year, we weren't going anywhere, and the reason we weren't going anywhere wasn't because of my dad's job or my mom's volunteer work or anything like that. We weren't going anywhere because we were having company - my cousin Ingrid. Her mom and step-dad were dropping her off on Friday after school and picking her up late Sunday, ten days later.

I was probably being selfish, but I groaned when I heard this. "Mom, I start college next year, when that happens I won't have the same spring break as Shannon and the boys. This is our last chance for a family vacation."

My mom was giving me that patronizing look she gets when I'm being over-dramatic. "Aine, it is not our last chance for a vacation together. In fact, we are already planning a lovely vacation for the summertime, when we can take more than a week. Your cousin is going through a hard time. We're giving her a place to relax while she's taking a break from stuff at home."

"Mom, this is Ingrid. She hates us. She probably doesn't want to come here anyway."

"I know she hasn't always gotten on well with us, but she seemed genuinely appreciative when we extended the invitation."

"Mom, ten days with Ingrid-"

"I know you'll manage it beautifully, Annie, and I think we have an opportunity to support and encourage your cousin."

I sighed.

"Thanks, Aine."

"Yeah, whatever."

Ingrid arrived on our doorstep on Friday afternoon at four o'clock. My mom was helping our church get ready for its annual Think Spring! Carnival, and Dad was in surgery. Tierney was at baseball practice, and J.D. was at my house, keeping Boyne and Shannon occupied by playing hackey with them in our large dining room (so much for spring break; it was under forty degrees outside, windy, dark, and rainy).

I walked to the side door, yanked it open, and admitted Ingrid and her stepfather, two of my least favorite people. Ingrid's stepfather, Joe Spinelli, was an "artist" and always wore black. He worked (on rare occasions) delivering pizza, and he was basically supported by my aunt. I told Ingrid and Joe Spinelli hello, and Joe grunted (he's not good with words) while Ingrid gave me an I-hate-it-here-but-at-least-it's-not-as-bad-as-home look.

I was getting ready a "clever" comment when something sobering popped into my head: Jesus saying, "Love your enemies and do good to those who hate you." A hard thing to swallow, yeah, but of all the words He used to describe the life of following Him, I don't think "easy" ever made the list.

I stifled a sigh, told Him I'd try, and took Ingrid's suitcase from Joe, wondering from the weight if she had stored pure gold inside. Ingrid tried to hand over the knapsack she was carrying, as well. "I don't think so," I told her. It was probably make-up, I thought as I shifted the suitcase to my other hand. It definitely wasn't clothes. Ingrid was wearing (in forty degree weather!) extremely short blue, denim cut-offs and a sequined bikini bathing suit top. I think my mom would rather have killed me than let me out of the house in get-up like that. Joe grunted a goodbye, and I opened the basement door and lugged Ingrid's suitcase down to the rec room. She followed me. After we dumped her luggage off, she looked at me. "Where is everybody?" she asked.

"Mom, Dad, and T.J. are out. Everyone else is in the dining room."

"Well, why aren't we in the dining room then?" Ingrid wasn't crazy about Boyne Andrew or Shannon, but she considered hanging with them better than being alone with me. I didn't want to be alone with her, either. I nodded and raced up the stairs to Andy, Shannon, and J.D. where it was safe (where I had corroborating witnesses no matter what I said later to my parents about what had happened to Ingrid Callahan).

J.D., Andy, and Shannon were resting when we got upstairs. J.D. was sitting cross-legged with his hands on his knees and Shannon on his lap. Andy was sitting beside them. The three of them were laughing softly, but when Ingrid and I walked in, they stopped. J.D. hooked an arm around Shannon's waist and stood (suspending her, giggling, in the air). Boyne came to stand by me. "Hey, Jay Dillon, you remember Ingrid?" I asked.

J.D. nodded and offered Ingrid his right hand to shake. She shook it, limply. Of course, she couldn't go an entire minute without being rude and felt compelled to ask my friend, "When did you move into this boarding house?"

"I don't live here," he said, matter-of-factly.

"Likely story." Her voice dripped sarcasm.

"Like you know anything," Boyne said, glaring at her. I put an arm around my little brother and ruffled his hair reassuringly. He's a brave kid, but he doesn't need to be the one fighting the family battles.

"Of course you knew J.D. doesn't live here," I told Ingrid, "you just wanted to make a nasty comment about my family.

Though I doubt my parents will be offended that you're accusing them of hospitality."

"You don't know what I was thinking. You're too stupid to even guess."

J.D. shook his head. "No, Aine's smart, and this time I'm sure she's 'spot on,' as it were."

"What do you know? You're stupider than she is."

He gave her an incredulous look. "Ingrid, if you want to get into a battle of insults with me, fine, but I can pretty much guarantee you won't win. I knew put-downs when I was six that you won't encounter in your entire life. The real difference is I don't take any of it personally anymore. Just…leave my friends alone." I gave J.D. a panicked look that warned him not to use any of said put-downs, but he wasn't looking at me.

"But you're both stupid. Look, you don't even know how to not dress like bums."

J.D. was wearing a pair of worn, but perfectly acceptable, jeans and a t-shirt that had a small rip in the right sleeve. I was wearing a sweatshirt and my favorite pair of ancient, patched and re-patched carpenter jeans. J.D. laughed, surprised at the bridge on which she'd chosen to stage her offensive. "Our clothes? You really wanna go there? Ingrid, are you unaware it's forty degrees outside, or is it just a new fad in Schaumberg to dress like a-?" He finally glanced at me, saw the warning look on my face and immediately suspended further commentary on her sense of style. It needed to be said, but my mom could handle it. It was kind of ironic, because even though Ingrid was more likely to take J.D.'s advice on immodest clothing than my Mom's, (he was, after all, an attractive teenage male) his saying it wasn't going to get me on Ingrid's good side. Besides, I could guess the word he was about to say, and that wasn't okay.

"Go ahead," Ingrid taunted him. "Say it. I dare ya." J.D. took his right arm and lifted my little sister up, so her head was level with his own. He was making the age-old "little ears" excuse. Shannon put her arms around his neck, leaned her head against his shoulder, and peeked at Ingrid from her safe spot. "What's the matter? You don't have a word for it in your three-year-old vocabulary?"

His speech impediment, the one thing that still bothered him. That was a bad moment for me; I had never hated anyone like that. I knew J.D. could take care of himself. He could do so much better than any lame insult she could throw at him. He could say a lot of things that wouldn't have been right to say, but he could've come up with some okay ones, too, things that might've been good for her to hear. But he wouldn't say any of them now, because of me. He could rip her apart with ninety-nine percent of his brain tied behind his back, but he wouldn't say a thing to her, and it was my fault. "That's my cue," he said, quietly. Reaching up, he loosened

Shannon's arms from his neck and returned her gently to the floor. He turned to a dining room chair, grabbed his jacket from it, and yanked it on. He reached for his keys on the table.

"I hate you!" Shannon told Ingrid.

"Shannon!" J.D. reprimanded sternly, and she hung her head. Then he was gone. No hug. No goodbye. Nothing.

He brushed past my mom on his way out, and she came in looking surprised and asked, "Why is J.D. leaving in such a hurry?"

"'Cause he's stupid," Ingrid said.

Mom looked at her. "Ingrid," she said. "Go put on actual clothes. Now."

Ingrid stormed off.

"What happened?" she asked me.

"Ingrid made him angry. He didn't want to tell her off, so he left to cool down."

"He was biting through his tongue, for sure," my mother commented.

Just then, Ingrid stormed back into the room, not wearing any more clothing. "My mom lets me dress like this!" she screeched. "You can't tell me what to wear!"

"Ingrid, I don't know what your mother lets you wear, but while you are staying in my house, you will not run around practically naked." Ingrid stomped away again. Mom sighed, pulled out a chair, and almost sat on J.D.'s backpack. "Oh, no," she said. "Well, you can give it to him on Sunday."

"I could give it to him tonight when Mark and I pick him up for the movie."

"Movie?"

"Yeah. We decided a few weeks ago to go out for movie night – right after we found out that Juli was going to visit her Dad, Amber would be with her grandparents, and Ben was going to Hank's grave. I asked you already. You said it was okay."

"I must've forgotten with all this going on with Ingrid. I'm sorry."

"Are you saying I can't go?"

"Well, will you take Ingrid with you?"

"Mom!"

"I know, there's friction between her and the boys, but you're really the best to entertain her. I'll call to clear it with Mark and J.D."

"They're not going to tell you they hate her, Mom."

"I'll ask them to be honest. Go make sure Ingrid looks decent. Loan her some of your clothes if she doesn't have anything."

I nodded, headed down to the rec room, then stopped. "Hey, Mom," I said. "Could you ask Mark if we could leave twenty minutes earlier, so I could get a chance to talk to J.D.?"

"Sure, honey."

"Thanks." I started off again. "*Alannah*," Mom called after me. I looked at her. "I really do appreciate this," she told me.

"Yeah. Thanks."

By the time Mark arrived, Mom and Ingrid had settled on a pair of my jeans and a baby tee she had in her bag. Ingrid wasn't happy with the outfit and sat in the back of Mark's van pouting while we drove to J.D.'s house. When we got there, Mark and Ingrid stayed in the living room with Jim and Karen while I went upstairs.

The door to J.D.'s room was open. J.D. was lying on top of the blankets on his bed with his eyes closed and his arms folded under his head. I stood in the doorway and tapped on the open door. He sat up quickly and looked at me. "Aine?" He looked at the clock on his nightstand. "You're early."

"I wanted to thank you for being so good today about my cousin."

"Right." He stood up and joined me in the hall. "I'm sorry about storming out," he said. "I don't know why, but she made me so angry, and I didn't know how long I could hold in all the things I wanted to say."

"She makes me feel the same way."

He smiled. "You really get me, don't you? I mean you understand what's up with me."

I shrugged.

"Hey," he said in mock protest. "I hold a copyright on that one."

I laughed, and he pulled me into his arms. "That's right," I said as I wrapped my arms around him. "I didn't get my goodbye hug this afternoon. I missed it."

"Me too." He picked me up and spun me around, and I giggled, feeling dizzy. When the dizziness passed, I found myself once again lost in his deep, bright blue eyes. He gave me an odd, confused look that disappeared when he bent his head. Everything was blurry for a second, so I closed my eyes right before our lips touched. After a moment, that seemed both terribly fleeting and totally everlasting at the same time, our lips parted. J.D. watched me for a second, looking amazed before that confused look returned. He let me go and pulled away. "I am…so sorry about that, Aine," he murmured. "I'm really sorry."

Now I felt confused. I didn't want him to apologize, but I didn't know what to say. "We should get going," he said. I nodded, dumbly, and followed him down the stairs.

When we got to the living room, Ingrid went up to J.D. to apologize like my mom had told her to do. Ingrid said, "Hey, J.D., look, I'm sorry for the way I acted today. It's just when you're angry, you look so hot."

My eyes widened. Standing behind her, Mark cringed. J.D. gave a little disbelieving laugh before turning to look at me and giving me a bug-eyed, gagging, oh-no-it's-Vanessa-all-over-again look. I tried my best to give my cousin a natural looking smile, and it was difficult, but I think I pulled it off okay, because Ingrid turned on her toes and sashayed towards the door.

As much as movies cost these days, I couldn't pay attention. I had a lot on my mind. Besides the Ingrid situation (which was big), I had to deal with the J.D. situation. It was confusing, to say the least. I had started to notice my feelings for him were changing. Ben had suggested the possibility that J.D. might be experiencing the same thing, but I hadn't imagined anything would happen like what had happened, at least not for a while. Sure, I'm eighteen, but I've been on two dates in my entire life. What I'm trying to say is this: that thing that evening with Jay Dillon…my first kiss. And, it had been…nice. But Ben had said J.D. would try to deny feelings for me, and I believed Ben was right. So where did that put us? J.D. pushing me away.

Not a single person we knew (with the possible exception of J.D. himself) would have hesitated to testify to the fact he'd grown up a lot emotionally within the past year-and-a-half. He was a lot more mature than the kid who'd had fallen out of the choir room ceiling. The only question was: exactly how much? I would have guessed he was fast approaching the level of emotional maturity possessed by your normal (stressed-out and slightly confused) eighteen-year-old human being. But I had nothing but my intuitions to support this theory. So, not only was I powerless to do anything, I wasn't sure I should.

I wished Juli were with me; she was better at the relationship thing. As much as I loved my mom, this was one situation I couldn't to explain to her. At that point J.D. didn't want my parents to know certain things, because he was afraid it could change how they viewed him. Mom didn't know about Keenan's attempted abuse of J.D., the time he'd given me the "get-me-anything?" speech while ditching class, the night he'd come into my room while high on ecstasy or the 'damaged goods' delusion. She'd only received the vaguest hints he'd used illegal drugs. Taking that into consideration, she was at a major disadvantage where any deeply personal conversation about J.D. was concerned. I needed to talk to someone who could help me get prepared for the talk I needed to have with J.D. Even Juli didn't know everything, neither did Mark. Only one person knew everything.

My dad was still at the hospital when we got home from the movie, and my siblings were in bed. My mom was exhausted, but she was waiting for us to tell her goodnight. When we saw her, Ingrid decided to argue about clothes again. The conversation didn't go well, and she ended up calling my mom an awful name. My mom sent her straight to bed. "You can stay up and read or something for a while," Mom told me. "But don't stay up too late. You've got a long day of entertaining Ingrid ahead of you." I groaned softly. She smiled at me, then her smile faded as she searched my face. "Is something wrong?"

"I'll be fine. Goodnight, Mom."

"'Night, *Alannah*." She went to bed. When she was gone, I went up to my room, grabbed my phone, took it into my walk-in closet, and closed the door. You learn a few tricks about privacy when you're growing up with three younger siblings, and one of the best was making phone calls from a closet. When a house has four kids, two parents, and tons of guests regularly going in and out, the only private places are closets and bathrooms, and I never took to taking phone calls on the toilet. In my closet, wrapped from toe to ear in a blanket, leaning on over a dozen cushions and pillows from my bed, chair, and window seat, I dialed the number.

It only rang once before it was answered. "Hello?" I heard.

"Hey, Aid. It's Annie. Whatcha doin'?"

"Watching television. You need to talk?"

"How did you ever guess?"

"One of your friends?"

"Um…sort of."

"Then it's gotta be about that 'drop-dead gorgeous,' blond guy you have a crush on and who has a crush on you."

"We kissed."

He gave a surprised, sputtering laugh. "When did this happen?" he asked.

"About four hours ago."

He whistled low and long. "As I recall, complications exist with the question of the two of you getting romantically involved."

"Yes. After… after it happened…"

"After you two lip-locked," he volunteered.

I giggled. "Yeah. After we kissed, he pulled away from me and apologized."

"Apologized? For kissing you?"

"Yeah."

"Wow."

"He has…"

"…issues. Your other friend was probably right, he probably thinks he's diseased."

"I've kind of got a problem."

"You kind of do."

"Any bright ideas?"

"Wait."

"Huh?"

"Wait. He needs to get himself together, you know. Wait for him to come around. If it's meant to be, he will come around."

"That's difficult, Aidan."

"I know, Annie. Brigid and I grew up together, but I was in love with her for six years before she'd go out with me." I sighed, and he went on, "She married me eight months later. That was a little quick, and I wouldn't necessarily advise that, but she'd lived across the hall from me for my entire life. I fell hard for this girl, you know. I even used to haul you and Tierney over to her apartment when your parents would bring you to visit, because I'd heard somewhere that girls liked guys who were good with kids."

"You used us!" I accused, teasingly. "To you, my brother and I were a pick-up line."

He laughed. "Meanwhile, I've been married for eight incredible years and have four beautiful children. I'm a stay-at-home dad and very happy."

"Your point?"

"It all works out. You are going to have a great life whatever happens. Just be patient, and trust God, because, believe it or not, He does know what He's doing."

"What about J.D.? What do I say to him?"

"Not much. You listen, mostly. It's delicate with J.D. because of all of the stuff that's happened to him. You shouldn't push him. Accept his feelings. But don't let him forget he's your friend, and you love him."

"What if he wants to put our friendship on ice?"

"Well, the friendship is worth fighting for. But, I'm going to warn you that after this, J.D.'s probably going to be more careful about physical contact with you than he has been recently. It's probably going to be a lot like it was before what happened last September. Remember the hugs and that are nice, for sure, but they can't be the most important things right now. Do stuff he's comfortable with, like the talks you've always had, movie nights..."

"You're right. About all of the above. Thanks, Aid."

"Anytime, wee one."

I giggled.

"And, until we meet again," Aid began.

I finished, "may God hold you in the palm of His hand." I held up my right hand in a fist and knocked lightly on the wood of my closet door, knowing Aidan was making the same gesture while knocking on his coffee table or something. If we had been parting physically, we would've knocked on each other's knuckles.

"Good night to you, Annie Eire," he said softly.

"And to you, Aidan D'éirinn."

I pressed the 'off' button on the phone, curled up on my pillows and cushions, and prayed, "Hey, God, I like this guy, but the big thing is I don't want to lose my friend."

I had just finished when the phone rang. I answered it, "Hello?"

"It was busy five minutes ago," I heard. J.D. had this habit of starting a phone call with a statement that sounds as if it belongs in the middle of a conversation.

"Yeah. I made a call."

"Let me guess: the only sane person in the universe besides you who answers the phone at midnight, Aidan O'Brien."

"It's only eleven there."

"Discussing your mutual dislike for your mutual relative?"

"Well, um…"

"Never mind. I'd love to hear all about it, but I've got a bit of a problem here on the home-front."

"What's that?"

"You and Aid's mutual relative."

"Huh?"

"Well, I'm sitting here in my room, and your cousin is throwing rocks at my window."

"I'll be right over." I didn't even stop to wake my mom. I'd tell my dad when he got home. I stepped into a pair of huarachis, pulled on a jacket, grabbed my keys, and headed out the door. The Jacobs house was on a corner, and they had only the backyard fenced, so I had a clear view of the west side of the house where Ingrid was standing (wearing the shorts and bikini top) and throwing asphalt pebbles at J.D.'s window.

I pulled up close to the curb, rolled down the window, and said, "Ingrid, get in the car." She looked at me and hesitated. "I am not repeating myself," I warned.

She frowned, walked over, and got into my car.

"Stay here while I go apologize to J.D. for letting you out of your cage." I got out, shut the door behind me, and ran across the yard to the front door. J.D. opened it before I could knock. Judging from the plaid, flannel pants, old t-shirt, and disheveled look he was wearing, he'd been trying to sleep when Ingrid stopped by. "I'm sorry about Ingrid," I said. "She's…"

"It's okay. I was just worried she'd wake my parents. They're still asleep, though."

"That's good." I paused, glancing down at my shoes before connecting back with his eyes. "Um, J.D. about what happened earlier-"

He interrupted me. "Don't worry. It won't happen again." I watched his eyes for a few seconds before he broke gaze with me. "Well, I hope your cousin will let you get some rest tonight," he said while staring down at his feet.

"Thanks. Good night."

He nodded, and I turned to go while he closed the door. Back in my car, I turned the key, kicked the brake pedal, and shifted the car into gear. "What were you thinking?" I asked Ingrid as I pulled out into the road.

227

"I thought he might like to go out and have some fun tonight."

"Want to know what everyone else thinks? That he doesn't like you and wants you to leave him alone and not wake his parents up in the middle of the night. Not to mention, you were sent to bed an hour ago for what you called my mother." She didn't respond, and everything was silent until we pulled into my driveway a few minutes later, about ninety seconds behind my dad. Dad watched us get out of the car.

"Where did you go? And why did you," he looked at Ingrid, "go to that place more than half-naked? And why did you," he looked at me, "go in your pajamas?"

"J.D. called me," I said. "She went over to his house to ask him to take her out on the town. She was throwing rocks at his window."

"Ingrid," he said, "go to bed." She disappeared into the house. My dad put his arm around my shoulder, and we started slowly up the steps together. "How's it going so far?" he asked.

"Well, in about eight hours, she's made J.D. so angry that he stormed out of the house biting his tongue so hard that it bled, made Mom angry three times, apologized to J.D. by saying he looked hot when he was angry, and broken curfew in an attempt to get J.D. to go bar-hopping with her, after she'd been sent to bed for calling Mom that one word everyone hates."

He sighed. "I'd trade her for Hannah, Micah, and both of the twins without a thought. I can only imagine how you feel."

"I'd let you throw in J.D.'s four nieces, his moody, pregnant sister, and her morning sickness, as well."

He laughed as he pulled open the door.

*****

Ingrid spent the next few days picking fights with my brothers and sister. On Saturday morning, Ingrid managed to get Boyne Andrew grounded before breakfast. He was trying to set the table, and Ingrid kept moving the silverware and dishes around on the table until he finally told her off.

She got Tierney in trouble on Sunday before church. While he was brushing his teeth, she kept turning off the water when he was rinsing his toothbrush. After she had done this about ten times, he finally sprayed her in the face with a bottle of her expensive hairspray. When my mom showed up, Ingrid had the nerve to chalk her behavior up to her being under house arrest for the weekend.

She got Shannon in trouble on Monday after taking Shannon's two favorite teddy bears and hiding them in the garden. When Shannon finally found Cheeseburger Blue and Boo Puddinpops, they were dirty and wet. Shannon called Ingrid a jerk and kicked her in the shin. Mom put Cheeseburger and Boo in the wash and grounded Shannon from television for a month.

I was thanked for taking Ingrid to the movies and dragging her home from J.D.'s house in the middle of the night. But it bothered me. I figured she was getting them in trouble because she couldn't get me, and that made me feel kind of guilty. I wanted it to stop.

Late Monday night, I was in a sleeping bag on the rec room floor, because, of course, Ingrid refused to stay in my room, and I had to keep her company. I was thinking about the situation. I squirmed around, rustling my blankets, and Ingrid shouted at me to be quiet because she was trying to sleep. That was all I was going to take from her. "What is wrong with you?" I asked her. "What are you so angry about that you absolutely must project on us?"

"Shut up," she said. "Your lives are perfect. You people have no idea what it's like."

"What's your big extinction-level disaster?"

"My mom's pregnant."

I wanted to knock her teeth out. Her Mom was old enough for complications to be a concern, but the birth of a child was definitely not the worst thing that could happen to a family. Besides, I doubted Ingrid's anger had anything to do with concern for her mother or the baby.

"What's the big deal?" I asked. It would be that she was embarrassed about her mother's pregnancy, or that the child would take up too much of her mother's time, or that she might have to help out around the house since her mother would be busy with the baby or that…

"It won't be Irish," she blurted.

Of course! The blind bigotry angle! That was perfectly reasonable. "Ingrid! Shame on you! That type of attitude is the reason our people have had so much trouble in the past."

"I have no problem with Italians," she said. "I just don't want any in my family."

"That is probably the most stupidly oxymoronic statement I've ever heard."

"No. I just mean, what if it joins the mob or something? I don't want a brother or sister who's in the mob."

"Ingrid, it's really hard to get into the mob if you weren't born in it, and I can guarantee you any who've done it didn't inherit their intelligence genes from Joe Spinelli."

"I'm going to have a mob boss for a baby brother or sister."

"I'm pretty sure you don't make Don status without being born in the mob."

"You're wrong."

"You're impossible. And you're being stupid. You can't really think this baby will join the mob. Your real reason is probably even more trivial, but less absurd."

"You're wrong again."

"Forget it. I can't do this now. I'm going to sleep."

"You're wrong."

"Be quiet. I'm trying to sleep."

*****

The rest of the week was just as miserable. My brothers and sister didn't get in any more trouble, but I was kept busy thinking up "fun" things to do with Ingrid. To make matters worse, I didn't see much of my friends because none of them could take Ingrid's personality.

We did hold our regularly scheduled video night (without Juliana, she didn't come back from Huntington Beach until the next day). Even that get-together was strained and uncomfortable with

Ingrid around. She babbled through five Cosby Show episodes about stuff that none of us wanted to hear.

And during that video night, I noticed J.D. had warped back into the psychological sunburn days with me. He play-fought with Mark and Ben, held my sister, and squeezed Amber's shoulder, but I didn't get my goodbye hug. I was glad he still showed to hang out with me, but after the bus crash I'd gotten used to giving all of my friends goodbye hugs (just because you never know). It was strange not including him anymore.

I have never before wished a school break would end, but I had been praying for this one to be over since Tuesday hit. If I hadn't been so tired by the time Joe finally came to get Ingrid, I would have thrown a party. As it was, I just crawled up the stairs and fell into bed.

Chapter twenty-eight –

After my graduation, my parents told my brothers, sister, and me about our summer vacation. Mom told us, "Juliana is going out to visit her dad in Huntington Beach for the whole month of June."

"She told us," I said.

"Back in February, when she and her father were planning her trip, they extended an invitation to her friends. Her father said a few of the houses near his were rented out on a short-term basis, as vacation homes. He said he could set up reservations if we wanted. The Wilsons decided to rent a house on one side of his, and the Jacobses and the Rosses are sending their boys with them. We are renting the house on the other side, and Amber's mom and step-dad have been kind enough to trust us with her."

"Really?"

"Yeah," my dad confirmed.

Shannon was jumping up and down. I knew she liked the beach, but I also figured she was excited about going on vacation with my friends. They all had the tendency to spoil my sister, which would mean a good trip for her. Tierney and Boyne Andrew liked the idea of the vacation (and my friends, too), but they were a lot more sedate about showing their enthusiasm.

"When do we leave?" Tierney asked.

"Three days," Dad told him.

Yeah, it was a hectic three days, and we didn't do much on the first day of vacation. We didn't even get to Huntington Beach until about seven in the evening (ten, Michigan time), and after the flight and the whirlwind of preparations preceding it, all we wanted to do was get the unpacking done and get some rest in our respective quarters.

The second day of our vacation dawned bright, fresh, and clear. I know this because for only about the second time in my life, I was up before the sun. I had woken up early feeling strangely energized, pulled on a bathing suit, cut-offs, and a t-shirt, and gone alone for a run along the shore in the dark. My feet pounded the sand where the water met the shore. Once the first hint of light had started to appear in the east, over the city, I had walked back to the house we were renting. I climbed the steps to the second floor deck in the back of the house. From the deck, I climbed onto the railing, hoisted myself to the roof, and watched the sun rise over the city. As the new day dawned in Surf City, I felt a sense of anticipation. I don't know if it was just graduating from high school, or if I somehow expected the events of the coming days, but I felt something about to change in my life.

Later that day, I hung out on the beach with my friends. We swam in the ocean, played volleyball in the park, helped my little sister build a sand castle on the shore, and ate a picnic lunch on blankets. For dinner, we went to a Hawaiian, surf restaurant near the pier at the City Beach. We watched the sun set over the beach, then Boyne and Shannon went to bed while Tierney, my friends, and I sat on Juli's porch and talked and laughed into the early morning.

The next day, I beat the sun out of bed again, and I took another run along the beach. I passed the spot where I'd gone hunting for sea-life with Boyne. I ran over the now-flat spot where my friends and I had helped my sister build that elaborate sand castle. I sprinted by the spot where we'd had our picnic lunch. I climbed the roof and felt again, with the sunrise, an even stronger sense of anticipation.

Twelve hours later all magic had evaporated. The whole group of us - Juli's dad, my family, Ben's family, all my friends - were having a barbeque. That wasn't bad. The food was great, and it was fun, until…

Well, we met a couple about our age, Nick and Jeanie, on the beach nearby and we invited them to our barbeque. They, their families, and a bunch of their friends were staying in a couple of the houses near ours. They seemed like nice people, and they didn't stay long enough to wear out their welcome. Before they left, however, Jeanie made an encouraging remark to J.D. and me. I don't remember exactly how she put it, but it gave the general impression that she thought J.D. and I were together - romantically speaking - but going through a fight of sorts. She basically said for us to suck it up, and it would pass. She said she and Nick, who were apparently dating or engaged, had made it through plenty of their own disagreements.

It wasn't her comment that upset me. On one level her statement seemed intrusive and presumptuous, but on another, it didn't. It was J.D.'s reaction to the statement and the jolting introspection which followed that upset me. J.D. stared after Jeanie as she and Nick walked up the beach. The two strangers disappeared around a bend, and J.D. gave me a forced-comical look and a statement of his own. "What on earth was that about?"

I forced a shrug, stood, and excused myself, my mind reeling. I hurried back to my family's rented house and the room I was sharing with Amber. As Jeanie's words had reached my brain, I had realized that recently J.D. had been withdrawing from me even more than he had immediately after the "incident" in the hallway. It was like he was retreating from our friendship. At the rate he was going, we'd be nothing but casual acquaintances by our second semester of college. After a growing closeness that had suddenly turned into strained distance, I imagined we had a particular way of relating to each other. It was probably this Jeanie had noticed. Maybe that could seem like a boyfriend and girlfriend having an argument to someone who didn't know (or perhaps, to someone who knew too well).

Anger, frustration, and sadness boiled in my heart that night. I didn't get up before the sun that next morning, and the pain only increased as the day went by. But Aid had said my friendship with J.D. was worth fighting for, and eventually in the afternoon, I declared war. I left my bunk and headed to the house where J.D. was staying with Mark and the Wilsons. I found him sitting alone at the picnic table on the back deck. A battery operated CD player blared grunge. He had a sketch pad in front of him, and a box of pencils, charcoal, and assorted erasers sat at his right elbow. He had tucked a stub of a pencil behind his left ear, and only the tip was visible underneath his blond hair. He was rubbing the pad of his left thumb around on his sketch pad, carefully blending the shadows in his sketch of the ocean.

"Hey, Jay Dillon," I greeted cheerfully.

He didn't look up. He just muttered a flat, distracted "hi."

"What's up?" I asked. No response. J.D. wiped his graphite-coated thumb on his denim-clad thigh, pulled the pencil from behind his ear, and made a few marks on his sketch. "Maybe I should light a couple of road flares on your table," I suggested.

He finally looked at me. "Aine," he said, "don't do this."

"Don't do what?" I asked, sarcastically. "Try to be friendly? Sorry. I forgot that was against the rules now."

The pencil slammed down on the sketchbook. J.D.'s right hand snapped backwards, sending the CD player flying. The player hit the deck, and the disc popped out of it and skated on its back across the boards and into the wall of the house. J.D. stood and stepped towards me. The look on his face scared me a little, and I backed away into the railing of the deck. He kept coming, and soon he was standing in front of me with his hands clamped painfully around my upper arms a couple inches beneath my shoulders.

"What do you want from me?" he shouted down into my face. I looked down. He went on in a slightly lower tone. "I'll give you anything you want," he said. "Magic words to absolve you of responsibility for me, my soul, my blood, money, anything, as long as you promise to leave me alone once you get it."

At first I couldn't believe what I was hearing, then I looked into his eyes and saw one of those things that maybe only God and I could understand about him. He was scared, and he was trying to scare me away so he didn't have to deal with the new fear. One thing I've learned is that some of the worst of the human condition is manifested out of fear. That's not an excuse, but it is one of the best keys to understanding other people (and yourself). "Jay Dillon," I said, "you know me better than that."

I could tell he felt guilty, but he didn't back off completely. He let go of my arms, and his voice dropped, but not much. "If you're under the impression that I need your help or something, you're delusional. I'm fine without you."

I looked nowhere but his eyes, because the person I knew was still behind them. "You do need me," I told him, "but even if you didn't, have you ever considered I need you?"

He laughed. When he spoke next, his voice was incredulous, "For what could you possibly need me?"

I didn't know how to say that I cared about him in the same way I believed he cared about me. I didn't know how to say that I believed the feelings he was running away from were the right thing for us. I didn't feel it was my place to say any of that. I stared at him with my mouth slightly open, ready to say words I couldn't find. He gave a humorless laugh and stepped back. As he backed up, I looked over his shoulder and saw Ben standing on the deck just outside the door to the house. He was watching the scene intently, probably had been for quite some time. Ben locked eyes with me for a second before turning to J.D. just as J.D., following my gaze, turned to look at him. J.D. broke eye contact with Ben quickly, turned back, sidestepped, flew down the staircase, and headed up the beach. Ben took off after J.D., and the two boys had their own charged discussion while I gathered up the CD player and disc and ran down the beach to my roof.

The CD player was a mid-priced AM/FM/Stereo model J.D. had picked up at a toy store in the mall back home. It was equipped with a clear, blue plastic lid that popped up when you pressed down on its right front corner. The lid had popped off entirely when the player hit the deck. I set the CD carefully back in the tray, locked the hinges on the lid back into place, and tried to put the lid down. Once I took my hand away, the lid popped open again, and I realized the latch had snapped during the fall. I held the lid down and pressed the player's power button. The player refused to power up, so I opened the battery slot in the back and shoved the loose batteries back into place, closing the circuit. This time the stereo powered up when I pushed the button. I held the lid down, and J.D.'s grunge music filled the air above the house.

Chapter twenty-nine ~

I didn't cry this time; I was too tired. I was amazed I'd found the strength to climb up to the roof and fix the CD player. I sat in that spot with my hands clasped over the stereo's lid, not crying. I had the player pulled so tightly to my stomach I could feel the buzz of the music coming from the speakers. While I sat huddled on the roof, I prayed in my head, and somewhere in the middle of a sentence, without meaning to, I fell asleep.

When I woke up, the CD had long since finished screaming J.D.'s grunge. The sun had disappeared, and twilight was chasing after it. I was still pushing the CD player's lid down with my hands. I had been pulled from my sleep by the rustling of clothes and the soft pounding of stocking feet as someone climbed the stairs and crossed the deck. I turned as J.D. pulled himself onto the roof.

He stood and started to walk across the roof, but he stopped when he noticed I was watching him. Even in the growing dark, he made a comical picture with his disheveled appearance. His socks and jeans were dark with water from his toes to his knees. His threadbare t-shirt was wrinkled and dusty with sand. His arms were spotted with goose bumps; a five o'clock shadow darkened his cheeks and chin. His eyes were red, and his hair was ruffled. He reached up to scratch his head, shaking sand from his windblown hair. After a moment, he sat down a couple feet in front of me. He looked at the stereo clutched against my abdomen. "Did I kill it?" he asked softly.

"The latch is broken," I told him. "The lid won't stay down on its own. I'm sorry."

He shook his head at me. "Don't be sorry," he advised. "I'm the one who had the temper tantrum. Duct tape will probably fix it, anyway."

I lowered my face down towards the player and closed my eyes. I heard the soft noises J.D. made as he scooted closer and settled beside me. "I'm sorry about that, by the way," he said. His words were nonchalant, but his tone was heavy. "I wouldn't pay you or...anything to leave me alone." I opened my eyes, but I didn't look up. "I don't want you to leave me alone," he continued. I could feel his eyes on my face, but I didn't look at him. He finally reached out his left hand, placed it under my chin, and gently guided my face so my eyes would lock with his. "You were right," he told me, dropping his hand. "I do need you."

I held back the tears threatening to spill from my eyes. J.D. watched me closely, leaning in just a little more. He could've kissed me, I realized, but he didn't. "Can I tell you something?" he asked.

I nodded.

"Today after Ben talked to me, I walked down the beach a little ways and sat down. Two little girls who must've been like four, a redhead and a curly-topped brunette, were building a sandcastle a few yards from where I was sitting. They worked on it for a long time, and it was nice. It had towers and windows; they dug a moat around it and used some sticks to make a drawbridge. But then the tide started creeping in. It got close to the castle, started washing away the moat, felling the little drawbridge. I got inexplicably upset watching this happen, so I looked at the two little girls and asked them, 'Aren't you going to build a wall to protect your castle?'

"And they looked at me with shock all over their little faces, amazed I would suggest such a thing. The redhead said to me, 'You can't fight the tide.'

"The little curly top nodded and said, 'It always comes, no matter what.'

"Nick, the guy from the barbeque the other day, came to get the little girls, and I thought for a while about what they had said. Then I fell asleep. I had a dream that I was lying on the beach, and the tide started coming in. I tried to get up, but I couldn't move. It took my feet, then my knees. It swallowed my waist and chest and crept in until I was surrounded by water, entirely washed away. Then I could move. I stood and was about to run from the water. Then I stopped, because I realized I was finally where I was supposed to be.

"I woke up, standing knee-deep in the ocean, covered in mud and missing my shoes, and I got it. Those little girls were right. 'Cause that's what I've been doing - with us, I mean - fighting the tide. But it doesn't work. The tide always comes." He paused for a moment and looked away before turning his eyes back to mine. "So," he said. "Here I am. If you'll have me."

I smiled softly and blinked away some more tears. "I'll take ya," I told him. He grinned, pulled me into his arms, and held me. In his arms, I realized something myself. Barring the day he'd fallen out of the ceiling into my choir room, I'd never seen J.D. looking so battered and scruffy. But he'd also never looked so good. When he let me go, we sat, silently, searching each other's eyes. Once again, he could've kissed me. But he didn't. He didn't have to.

Chapter thirty –

About a week after coming back from Huntington Beach,
J.D. and I went on our first official date. We were missing the
beach, so we went back – not to Surf City, of course, but a local one.
He picked me up after dinner, and we walked down the pier and got
back just as the sun was beginning to set. We watched the sky for a
while, and I took a few pictures. It started to get cold, so we didn't
stay long after the sunset began. We went to State Street Joe's to
drink cappuccino, eat cookies, and talk. It wasn't anything fancy,
but it was a lot of fun. It had been a while since the two of us had
laughed together like we did that evening.

I was glad to get my hugs back, too, and J.D. was good about
giving me plenty of those within the next eight weeks or so. In mid-
August, I got a big goodbye hug (and a little kiss, too), because we
wouldn't be seeing each other until college in Boston. Jim and
Karen had gotten a call from Kieran in Detroit, because Hope, J.D.'s
fifth niece, had arrived. Mr. and Mrs. Jacobses took J.D. to spend a
few weeks with the family. He called me the first night with stories
about his nieces, and we laughed together for nearly an hour before
saying goodbye.

J.D. was still in Detroit a week before we started college, when my family got on a plane to Boston. We were going to stay at O'Reilly's, the inn my mom and sister had fallen in love with a year before. Shannon was excited about seeing her friend Crea again. The two little girls had exchanged a few letters since they had met, but they weren't great writers yet; Crea was only in kindergarten, and Shannon wasn't much older.

We got to O'Reilly's around one in the afternoon. The desk was deserted, except for one the cutest little girls I had ever seen. Blonde hair, blue eyes, dimples…and somehow, she kind of seemed familiar. The chair behind the desk was a swivel chair, and she was spinning in it, around and around and around. When Shannon saw the little girl, she shouted her name and ran toward her. Crea saw Shannon, slid down out of the chair and hurried around the counter. The little girls hugged and chatted excitedly while my parents stepped up to the counter and looked around. "Oh!" Crea said suddenly. "I needta get Grampa." She scurried back behind the counter, climbed the chair, and pressed a button that was behind the cash register.

A voice came out of the air, "Check-ins or check-outs, sweetheart?"

"Check-ins. It's Shannon and her family."

"Oh! I will be right out."

Crea looked up. "See, one of our waitresses walked off yesterday," she explained. "Our desk-girl is helping in the restaurant 'cause we got a big party today. Grampa set me up here and told me to call him in his office when customers needed helping. I can page the bellhop. He'll bring in your luggage if you show him to your car. Want me to?"

"Sure," my dad said.

Crea picked up the phone, called a speed dial number, waited a moment, and hung up. "Our bellhop carries a beeper while he's here," she told us. "So no matter where he is now, he'll be here soon."

Mr. Kavanagh, a friendly-looking, sixtyish man with blue eyes and full head of gray hair, arrived a few seconds later. The bellman was close behind his boss. Mom checked us in while Dad and the boys went to help the bellman haul the luggage. "I'm sorry about the wait, Mrs. O'Brien," Mr. Kavanagh apologized as he programmed several electronic key cards to open the doors of suites 287 and 289.

"It's okay," Mom said. "Crea was telling us you've been having trouble with your help."

"Yes. More of my summer help left than usual, so I was already short-staffed. When that waitress walked out on her shift yesterday, it…"

"It all came tumbling down," Crea sing-songed with a smile.

"Exactly." Mr. Kavanagh looked at me and smiled. "I don't suppose you're looking for a job?" he teased. "Decent pay, and the summer's our busy season, so the rest of the year, I offer free room and one meal and a snack everyday to my help if they want it. The kitchenette suites are very nice."

I was looking for a job. "Seriously?" I asked him.

He looked at me. "An interview?" he suggested. "Tomorrow at eleven? In my office?"

"I'll be there."

"See you then," Mr. Kavanagh said. "Meanwhile, have a nice evening." He handed over our key cards and smiled.

*****

That night we had pizza delivered from a local Italian restaurant, and we watched a movie on cable while we ate pepperoni and extra cheese and drank bottle after bottle of Coke. After the movie ended, I took Shannon down to the pool for a swim. Crea was supposed to join us later, but at that time on that Tuesday night, my sister and I were the only ones in the entire rec center. We raced, splashed each other, and played games until we tired ourselves out. Then we got out of the pool, wrapped ourselves up in the small, fluffy, pale-green towels O'Reilly's kept for their customers, and sat on the edge of the pool with our legs dangling into the water. "That was fun," Shannon told me, but she sounded gloomy.

"Yes, it was a lot fun," I agreed with her. "We should do this more often."

Just like that, she burst into tears. "We can't!" she blurted. "You won't be around!"

"Shannon," I said, putting my arm around her. "I won't be out here all the time. I'll come back for breaks. Besides, I won't be in college forever."

"Yeah, but you're not coming back home when you finish college. You'll stay here, or go somewhere else."

"Shannon…"

"I don't blame you, Aine. I'll probably move someplace else too. So will T.J. and Boyne Andrew. We all go off – that's life – I just hate it now that it's happening."

"I'll miss you, too, Shannon, but I'll always be your big sister, and I'll always love you with all my heart."

"I know that, but it's still hard."

"It'll get easier. When we have our own great separate lives, we'll realize they're enhanced by the relationships we've shared since we were small."

She had stopped crying, but she gave me a confused look. "I'm nine," she reminded.

"Dad and Aid grew up together, but now Dad has Mom, T.J., Boyne, you, and me, and Aid has Brigid, Hannah, Micah, and the twins, and all of us have great family relationships together. When we're older and have families of our own, our sister friendship will be like this great bonus. The love grows with the family. See?"

"I guess. Sorta."

I smiled. "Never mind that, though. Just know it gets better than it is now."

She gave me a lopsided smile, and I dipped my thumb in the pool and wiped away her drying tears. She gave me a hug just as the rec room door opened and Crea came skipping toward us. Crea was wearing blue denim bib-alls over her bright blue bathing suit. "We gonna swim?" she asked. "Grampa said I could swim without him since you were here to watch, Aine."

"Yeah," I told her. "We're gonna swim."

After Crea tired Shannon and me out for the second time, we settled on some of the poolside lounges and talked. Crea asked us about our family and told us about hers.

"Gramma, Grampa's wife died when my mom was little," she said. "Grampa talks about her a lot. He's got lots of good stories."

"What about your parents?" Shannon asked.

"My mommy, Aisling, disappears." Crea explained ("Aisling" is pronounced ASH-ling). "She left for a long time, came back, and had me here; then she left again, and I don't remember her or my brother. My mom left when I was little, and my brother died when he was six, when I been really little, I guess 'cause I do remember Mommy's voice at least, but not him at all."

"What about your daddy?" Shannon asked.

Crea shrugged. "I guess I don't have a daddy."

"Everyone's got a daddy. You don't get babies without Daddies."

"Maybe he died when I was little, too. I don't know him."

"Maybe he doesn't know you either," I suggested.

"Maybe. I have Grampa, though. Grampa's great." She grinned, and my sister and I couldn't help smiling back.

Chapter thirty-one –

Mom woke me up at nine-thirty the next morning and handed me the telephone. I scooted to a sitting position and said hello into the mouthpiece.

"Hey, Annie."

"Oh, hi, Jay Dillon."

"Did I wake you up?" he asked.

"Yes, but it's okay. I have to get up, anyway. I have a job interview at eleven that I have to get ready for."

"A job interview?"

"It's here, I mean, at the Inn. I'd be a waitress, I think. And it's a nice restaurant, so the tips would be good. Mr. Kavanagh said I could live in the hotel and get some of my board here for free, plus a good hourly wage."

"That's a good deal."

"Yeah. I think Mr. Kavanagh is looking to hire more than one person, so maybe you could fill out an application when you get here on Friday morning."

"Maybe I will. Though I probably won't have a lot of time before orientation."

"Well, I could get an application for you and even fill out most of it."

He laughed. "Okay, Annie."

"Are you still in Detroit?" I asked him.

"No, we just got home. I'm glad. I mean, I love the girls, but they have more energy than human beings have any right to, especially ones so small."

I giggled. "What do you think of baby Hope?"

"She's sweet. She's kind of…funny-looking, all red and wrinkly."

"That's what newborn babies look like, J.D."

"That's what Mom said, but how would I know?"

"You wouldn't," I agreed, then asked, "How's Shelby?"

"Great," he said. "We had a lot of fun playing together." I could hear the grin in his voice. J.D. loved all of his nieces, but he definitely had the most fun with Shelby.

"Are you tired?" I asked him.

"Yeah. I was going to take a nap this morning before I started packing for college."

"I'll let you go, then, but I'll see you in a couple days."

"Yeah. I'll probably call you again, too, if that's okay?"

"Of course. I'd like that."

We talked for a little longer before saying goodbye. I'd slept kind of late, so after I hung up with J.D., I hurried to grab some breakfast and get ready for the interview. I was a little nervous about it, but it went well. When Mr. Kavanagh told me the wage he was offering, my jaw dropped. "Even for waitressing?" I asked. "That much?" Niamh's was a nice restaurant. I expected the tips would be good.

"Well," he said, "you'll be trained to help with the counter, snack bar, and other things. Your main job will be waitressing, but if you get called away from it, you're not making tips. It's not fair to you to make a very low wage if you're not getting the other compensation."

"That's more than fair."

"I try." He smiled at me and looked down at the application I had handed him. I fidgeted nervously while he studied it. To occupy my mind, I glanced around Mr. Kavanagh's office for interesting things. The east wall featured a window that looked out over a flowery courtyard with old-fashioned park benches sitting along the brick-paved walk. The south wall sported a VanGogh print. The desk, the chairs, and the cabinet were all beautifully crafted mahogany. A gold-plated sign with the name "Mr. Jonathan D. Kavanagh" printed on it in fancy script was sitting in the middle of his desk. Mr. Kavanagh's pencil cup was a ceramic one with a big yellow smiley face on it (hand-painted by Crea, I guessed). Three framed snapshots sat on the end of Mr. Kavanagh's desk. These were facing outward, in the showoff position. He had others facing him, but these were "pride pieces," as my Dad would have said. I leaned forward to get a better look at the photographs.

The picture on the end was an older photograph of a teenaged girl whom I assumed was Mr. Kavanagh's daughter, Crea's mom, Aisling. In her face, I saw the same phantom of familiarity I had noticed when I looked at Crea for the first time. The picture had been taken in the garden in front of the Inn. Aisling was a pretty girl with long, strawberry blonde hair and bright blue eyes. It was a beautiful, sunny day, and she was laughing at something. In this picture she didn't look like the dysfunctional person who would later disappear and come back only to leave her daughter in Mr. Kavanagh's care.

The second picture was of Crea. It had probably been taken sometime within the last few months. Crea was dressed in a pale blue, flowered sundress and posed on a park swing. She was grinning for the camera, and she looked a lot like her mom.

The third picture was of a blond-haired, blue-eyed, three-year-old boy. My eyes first gave the child a nonchalant glance, but as I took in the face, it locked me into a stare. I had seen it before. I mean, it wasn't the same photo, but it was the same little boy. Before I could stop myself, I was out of my seat, and the framed photo was clutched in my hand. Mr. Kavanagh looked up at me and stared on in surprise. "Aine?" he asked.

"This little boy," I murmured.

"That's my grandson," he told me. "He would be turning nineteen tomorrow, but he died from cancer when he was six."

"Who told you that?"

"My daughter Aisling. His mother."

"She lied."

"Excuse me?"

"She lied. He's not dead. He's fine. At least he was an hour-and-a-half ago."

"You must be mistaken."

"No, it's him. It's him, see…" I set the frame down, grabbed my purse from under the chair, and pulled out my wallet. I opened it and leafed through the photo plates. "Here," I said once I'd found the one I wanted. I held the picture out to him. "It's the same kid," I told him. I turned his photo so he could see them both side-by-side. "It's the same kid," I repeated.

"How did you get a picture of my grandson? Crea wouldn't have…She knows so little about her brother, she doesn't even have an accurate concept of when he died."

"No, no, no. Look," I flipped the photo plate. "Here he is in kindergarten. And when he was ten." I flipped it again. "This was taken about three weeks ago."

Mr. Kavanagh stared at the photos.

"His middle name is Dillon, and his first name starts with a J., but that's all we know, that's all he was able to tell us. He talks strangely, doesn't pronounce r's and l's very well, like he…"

"…He's from Boston," Mr. Kavanagh finished. He looked up at me. "He and his mother lived right here with me in O'Reilly's until he was three." Mr. Kavanagh blinked, looking dazed. "Jonathan," he continued. "His name is Jonathan Dillon Kavanagh. Aisling gave him my name. We never called him Jonathan, because I'm Jonathan. I wouldn't have been surprised if he got to age three without knowing his first name."

Mr. Kavanagh fingered the most recent picture. I had taken it in my mom's garden a few weeks before. It was a great picture. The day was beautiful, and J.D. was smiling, and he looked gorgeous. "He's been in Michigan?" Jonathan Kavanagh the elder asked me.

"Yeah," I answered.

"Foster care?"

I nodded.

"I would've kept looking for him if she hadn't told me he was dead."

"You looked for him?"

"Well, mostly for her, but he was supposed to be with her. People aren't supposed to leave their kids…"

"He was found in an alley," I said.

"An alley? Oh…" He groaned softly and frowned.

Something clicked in my head. The name "Aisling" was Gaelic for vision or dream. "You're 'dreamsearch'?" I asked.

He looked at me, surprised, and nodded. "You saw the posting?"

"Yes. Me and my friend Mark. We sent you the youngest picture we had of J.D., but the account had been canceled."

"She'd come back," Mr. Kavanagh said, "and she'd told me he was dead."

My mind whirled…Jay Dillon Foster…No, Jonathan Dillon Kavanagh, the younger, was having a birthday tomorrow. Not October 24th – August 31st. "Would you like to see him?" I asked.

"I would. His birthday…"

"May I use your phone?"

He was already pushing it my way.

Chapter thirty-two ~

I had never felt as impatient as I did right then, waiting for someone - anyone! – at J.D.'s house to pick up the phone. I drummed my fingers through the three agonizing rings.

"Hello?"

"Mrs. Jacobs, it's Aine. May I talk to J.D.?"

"Well, Annie, J.D.'s in his room trying to get a little sleep."

"Would you please wake him up? This is really important."

"Well, Annie…"

"Please. You know I wouldn't usually ask."

"All right. Hang on." I went through another miserable wait. Finally, I heard the sounds of J.D. (half asleep) picking up (and dropping on the floor and fumbling with and picking up again) the receiver of his telephone. "Hello?" he said, sounding a little blurry.

"Hey, Jay Dillon. Are your plane tickets exchangeable?"

"Huh? Why?"

"Are they?"

"Yeah. I think so."

"Can you fly out here tomorrow morning?"

"Why?"

"I don't want to tell you over the phone, but it's important. You won't be disappointed if you come."

"Aine, it's just one day early."

"But tomorrow's a special day."

"How so?"

"I wanna tell you in person. Please, J.D." J.D. didn't respond right away.

Jonathan Dillon Kavanagh, the elder, handed me a note. It said, "I'll arrange and pay for tickets." I wrote, "His foster parents?" on the note. "Please, if they will," he wrote back.

"J.D., the tickets will be covered," I blurted. "For your parents, too, if they'll come. I'll call you tonight with the information, and you'll just have to cancel the tickets you have and pick up the new tickets at the airport tomorrow morning."

"Aine, what is this about?"

"Come on, J.D. A free trip to Boston. You can take the refund money for your next semester's tuition, or a holiday trip home."

"Aine…"

"J.D., please, trust me on this."

He didn't respond right away. Finally, he sighed and said, "Well, I guess I have some packing to do."

"Thanks, J.D. You won't regret this."

"Yeah, well, we'll see. Remember, I can't answer for my parents."

"Yeah, I know. But you'll ask them?"

"Yeah. I'll see you tomorrow, Aine."

"Yeah. See ya, J.D."

Mr. Kavanagh called his travel agent and arranged for three tickets on a nonstop flight from Detroit Metro to Logan in Boston for the next morning. I called J.D. back and told him the arrangements. He told me he had - just barely - convinced his parents to come. "They weren't going to come to college with me," he said. "They didn't know why they suddenly had free tickets. Who's paying for this, anyway?"

"The owner of the Inn."

"Why?"

"J.D."

"Right, right. Not over the phone."

After I hung up, Mr. Kavanagh looked at me. "Is he okay?" he asked.

"Yeah," I said, "he's fine. I'm not going to lie to you; he's been through some bad stuff. Almost two years ago, though, he got placed in a good family that loves him. Now he has two great parents, four sisters, two brothers-in-law, and five nieces."

Mr. Kavanagh gave me a weak smile. He corrected, "He has five sisters."

"He does at that," I agreed, smiling and thinking of little Crea.

We both sat lost in our thoughts for a moment. "So," I finally asked. "Now what?"

"Tell your family I asked you to invite them to my grandson's birthday party tomorrow afternoon. I mean…"

"They don't need to know before he does."

"Exactly."

"I'll do that."

"And I'll tell my staff to organize a party." His blue eyes were twinkling. "You'll have to tell him," he told me. "If I see him, I won't be able to tell him, and he'll wonder why this strange old man is trying to give him a hug."

"Okay."

"Well, we have work to do. I should explain to my granddaughter, too."

I nodded, stood, and turned to go.

"You're hired, by the way," he called after me.

"Thanks, Boss," I called back.

Crea was in our hotel room playing with my sister when I told my family Mr. Kavanagh had asked me to invite them to his grandson's birthday party. "My brother?" Crea asked.

"I guess," I told her.

"But he's dead."

I shrugged. "I can only tell you what your Grampa told me to tell my family. You could talk to him, though."

"I think I should," she said, standing up to go.

Crea waved goodbye and headed out the door. When she was gone, Mom looked at me. "Is this some kind of ceremonial birthday party for his dead grandson, or does he have another grandson who's actually having a party?"

"Mr. Kavanagh asked me just to invite you to his grandson's birthday party."

"Should we get a gift?"

I shrugged. "It couldn't hurt, I guess. We could always return it."

"True enough. Did he tell you how old his grandson is – or would be if he were alive?"

"Nineteen, I think."

"You want to go shopping with me? You have a better idea what a nineteen-year-old would like as a present than I would."

"Um…" I faltered. "Sure."

Chapter thirty-three –

I was waiting on the front walk when the cab carrying J.D., Jim, and Karen pulled into O'Reilly's loading/unloading zone. They got out of the car, unloaded their bags, and joined me at the curb. As the cab drove away, three skeptical faces examined mine. The scrutiny made me want to squirm. "Mr. Jonathan Kavanagh, the owner of the Inn, wanted you to come to his grandson's birthday party," I explained lamely as I led them inside. They gave me yeah-right looks. They hardly noticed when the bellhop came for their luggage. I pointed Mr. and Mrs. Jacobs to the doorway at the north end of the lobby, which led to Niamh's. "You two may join the party," I told them. "I have to show J.D. something."

They headed to the restaurant. I took J.D.'s hand and pulled him in the general direction of the restaurant. Before we got to Niamh's, we hung a right into Mr. Kavanagh's office.

"Why does Mr. Jonathan Kavanagh want me at his grandson's birthday party?" J.D. asked me as we entered. "I don't know this guy or his grandson."

I closed the door to the office. "How was your flight?" I asked him.

"It was fine. But, Aine…"

"You don't know him," I admitted, "but he knows you."

"Who?"

"Jonathan Dillon Kavanagh, Mr. Kavanagh's grandson."

"But, really? Aine, this guy dragged me halfway across the country, but I have no recollection of him whatsoever. How well can he know me?"

"I don't know," I said. "How well do you know yourself?"

"What kind of question is that, Aine?" He was getting a little frustrated with me, I could tell. "I want to know what's going on."

I shrugged and had him sit in one of the mahogany-framed, upholstered guest chairs. I leaned against the edge of the desk and picked up the framed snapshot of not-quite-three-year-old Jonathan Dillon Kavanagh. He looked down at the photo then at me with utter confusion on his face. "Look familiar?" I asked, gently.

"It looks kinda like the baby picture of me you keep in your wallet. But I don't see…"

Yes, Jay Dillon was acting dense, and it annoyed me a little. But I guess I understood it, as well, like I understand most things about him. With many people, when they go through unexpected tragedies, they often feel denial. They go through a shocked, "This is not happening; this is not happening…" phase. I felt a little bit of that after the bus crash.

But I guess, when the tragedy is not so sudden, it's a little different. If you're nineteen, and that tragedy has lasted for sixteen years, it could become an integral part of your life. It would be all you know, so if a tragedy like that finally ends, your life without it can seem strange and surreal. I think that's what happened. J.D. didn't understand right away, because part of him was reeling with shock and saying, "This is not happening; this is not happening..."

"Come on," I said, taking his hand again. He gripped my hand and followed me through the door on the north side of the office, through a hallway, and into the restaurant where more than a dozen people sat, mostly looking confused. I pointed at a banner hanging from the ceiling in front of us. "Happy Birthday, Jonathan Dillon Kavanagh!" it read.

"Happy birthday, J.D.," I told him, softly.

"My birthday isn't for two months, Aine," he corrected.

"Not your designated birthday, Jonathan Dillon. Your real birthday." Then it sunk in. Jonathan Dillon Kavanagh, the younger, smiled as a few tears appeared in his bright baby blues.

*****

After the party, Mr. Kavanagh showed me my second floor kitchenette suite. Then he took us up to the fourth floor, where he offered J.D. the suite across the hall from his own living quarters. While J.D. got to know his grandfather and his little sister, I went back to my room and picked up the phone to give our friends the 4-1-1. Mark ended up being the last one I got a hold of, and I could hear the grin in his voice. "Wow," he said. "Imagine that. The big search is over; you found him." I laughed then, but I'm not sure he was exactly right.

One night after all the hype, after J.D. got to know and love his grandfather and baby sister, he and I were sitting in the deserted pool room talking about everything that had happened.

I said, "I guess Jay Dillon Foster is the one who's lost now."

"I don't think so," he responded. "Remember how Ben chased me down the beach after you and I had that fight last summer?"

"Sure. You guys argued."

"He grabbed me, and I told him to leave me alone. He said no and told me I was a fool.

"I told him, 'You guys don't get it. I'm fine. I don't need anything.'

"He said, 'You might want to check in with Jay Dillon Foster, see what he needs, because he needs someone who'll understand him. If you can't see that, you're a fool. You're also a fool if you can't see Aine O'Brien is the only person on the face of the earth who fits that description. And the fact that I "don't get it" only reinforces that truth.'"

J.D. paused thoughtfully for a moment, smiled, and went on, "I'll never lose that, Annie. I'll always need you.

An Críoch

Acknowledgements

I penciled my first "novel" at the age of seven, and so many people have helped and encouraged me over the years. I know I won't hit on half of those, but I thought I'd try.

Thanks are owed to Dad and Mom, Jeremiah and Alex, my grandparents. To Sarah, Caro, Monkey, Beck, Brit, Ross, Jeana, Dawn, Ricky, and G.C.S. for inspiration. To Amy, my copy-editor. To Ryan, our "hand model". To Con, for the Irish. To all the pray-ers who kept me going for so many years.

And most especially to my Best Friend who never leaves, the Breath who keeps me alive, the Dream Giver who, one night several years ago, showed me a bus. You are good. All the time.

Drafted September 10, 2001 10:10 p.m.
Revised November 18, 2006 10:26 a.m.
Críochnaithe October 23, 2008 1:15 p.m.
Mason, Michigan.

~Raelee May Carpenter
Always.
Forever.
He is God.

Printed in the United States
209000BV00003B/1-105/P